Amy Cross is the author of more than 200 horror, paranormal, fantasy and thriller novels.

THE FIFTH TOMB

THE CHRONICLES OF SISTER JUNE BOOK FIVE

AMY CROSS

This edition
first published by Blackwych Books Ltd
United Kingdom, 2023

Also available in e-book format.

www.blackwychbooks.com

CONTENTS

THE

FIFTH

TOMB

PROLOGUE

1981...

GASPING BREATHS COULD BE heard coming
from somewhere in the darkened room, as Cardinal
Boone stopped at the doorway and looked through.
Bathed in the brightness of the corridor, he watched
the darkness and felt a shudder pass through his
chest.

"Penny for them?"

Sighing, he turned and saw Cardinal
Abruzzo approaching from the other direction.

"Almost beat you to it," Abruzzo continued,
stopping at the doorway and looking into the room,
where the only light could be seen around the edges
of the blackout curtains. "How was she last night?"

"I haven't had a chance to ask anyone," Boone explained, before pausing for a few seconds as the rasped breaths continued. "She's alive, at least. Given her condition, that has to count as a miracle."

"I do not like to witness such suffering," Abruzzo explained. "After everything she has done for our cause, I sometimes wonder whether it's right for her to cling on in this manner."

"I hope you're not suggesting -"

"I'm not suggesting anything," Abruzzo continued, interrupting him. "I'm merely observing that sometimes, after a lifetime of service, the time comes for a faithful servant to... let go. I pray for her continued survival, of course, like everyone else, but sometimes I worry that such prayers are counterproductive."

"She'll never let go," Boone told him. "Not while she has any say in the matter, at least. She has always been so firmly focused on the task at hand, and sometimes I swear she intends to deny death itself if that's what it takes. For so long now she has been insisting that the moment of glory is close, and I have no doubt that she believes this to be true. She might be right or she might not, but the belief keeps her going."

They stood in silence for a moment,

listening as the groaning breaths continued.

"Even," Boone added, "long past the point at which anyone else would have accepted the inevitable." He paused, staring into the room again, before turning to Abruzzo. "Why are you here, anyway? You don't usually come to trouble her unless you want something for yourself."

"Cynicism does not suit you," Abruzzo replied. "You should take sin care to include that in your next confession."

"What are you doing here?" Boone asked again. "Cut the clever talk and just be honest."

"I have some news to deliver regarding the mission," Abruzzo explained. "Of course, if you would rather deliver it yourself, then I will happily give you that honor."

"Is it good news or bad news?"

"That has yet to be determined."

"Then I think the honor should remain all yours," Boone muttered, taking a step back. "Last time I even dared to speak to her, she damn near bit my head off. Call my cynical all you want, but age and ill health don't really suit her. Just take some friendly advice and don't get too close to her bed. She had her walking stick lengthened recently. And sharpened."

With that he turned and walked away, and

his footsteps rang out as he disappeared into the distance, leaving Abruzzo to turn and look once more into the darkened room.

"Who's there?" a frail female voice called out. "I know someone is at my door! I demand to know who it is!"

***

"Are you sure?" Sister Josephine asked, her weakened and rasping voice sounding particularly bare in the darkness. She shifted a little, and the bed creaked beneath her insubstantial weight. "You should not come to me with this news if you're not sure."

"I've checked and re-checked," Abruzzo replied, standing at the foot of the bed, one side of his face slightly picked out by a sliver of light. "Obviously it's impossible to be certain right now, but so far all the signs are looking very good. I expect to receive confirmation within a week."

"How?"

"I have sent our best agent to investigate."

"Who?"

"I think you know who."

Abruzzo waited, and after a few seconds he heard a faint ripple of laughter coming from the darkness ahead; after a few more seconds this laughter was interrupted by a series of coughs, and a moment longer passed before the coughs came to a spluttering halt.

"How very appropriate," Sister Josephine chuckled. "I must admit, Abruzzo, that you have a certain... artistic flourish when it comes to these things."

"I try my best."

"You were right to come to me so soon," Sister Josephine continued. "I want to be kept completely up-to-date about every development. Do you understand me? I don't care what time it is, day or night, I want to know as soon as you have any news. Even if that stupid doctor tells you to leave me alone, make sure you reach me. Kill the idiot if you have to."

"I would hope that it won't come to that," Abruzzo said delicately.

"As soon as we have confirmation, I want to get out there," she told him. "I don't care how difficult it might be to make the arrangements, I want to be on the jet within half an hour of the confirmation coming through."

"Your doctor -"

"I don't care about doctors and their moronic opinions!" she hissed, and now she sounded increasingly frustrated. "Were you even listening to me a moment ago? Do I have to kill that doctor myself, just to make you stop listening to him? This could be the culmination of a lifetime's work, not to mention the work of so many generations before us. If we have indeed found one of the gates, then I demand to be there!" She let out an exhausted sigh, accompanied by the sound of the bed creaking a little more. "Leave me now," she continued. "You've given me much to think about. As soon as Sister June delivers her report, I want to be informed about its contents. Do you understand?"

"Of course," he replied, before turning and heading to the door. "I shall pray for our hopes, so that -"

"How is she getting there?"

Stopping in the doorway, he turned to look back across the darkened room.

"To the desert, I mean," Sister Josephine continued. "You haven't let her use the jet, have you? I hope I made it very clear that I want her to suffer as much as possible on these journeys. Second class all the way. Third class, if such a thing exists. Long layovers. Terrible food. That sort of thing."

"Oh, I think a degree of discomfort is certain on this occasion," he said with a faint smile.

"I myself booked her a particularly uncomfortable seat on an airline with a terrible reputation. I even contacted them to make sure that she has a seat with very little legroom."

"And how is she getting to the site?"

"I considered having her driven out there in a vehicle," Abruzzo explained, "but... then I came up with an option that seemed to be more in line with your requests." He checked his watch. "In fact, around about now, Sister June should be feeling distinctly out of sorts."

CHAPTER ONE

THE CAMEL STUMBLED BRIEFLY, its body jerking enough to make June grip the reins extra firmly. Momentarily worried that she might be about to fall off, she tightened every muscle in her body, only for the camel to let out a faint grunting noise and continue on its way across the dunes.

The shepherd, riding another camel just a short way ahead, glanced back at her and smiled. He said something in a language June didn't understand – in a language that didn't really sound, to her, like a language at all – and then he looked ahead again.

"I'm sorry?" June said, raising her voice a little in the hope that she might be heard. "I beg your pardon? As I explained back in the town, I don't speak -"

Stopping suddenly, she didn't even realize the name of the language, and she felt not only hopelessly lost but also rather ignorant. She knew *where* she was, out in the desert in a disputed area near Morocco, but otherwise she'd barely had time to get accustomed to her surroundings at all; the plane ticket from the First Order had been couriered to her at the very last minute, leaving her with barely enough time to pack a bag. Two days earlier she'd been safely ensconced in her office at the convent, and now she was under the harsh desert sun, dressed in her habit but with an extra shawl pulled over the top of her head to protect her from the sun.

Ahead, the other camel came to a halt at the top of the dune, and the shepherd began to climb down.

"Is everything okay?" June asked, a little confused as the man made his way over. "Is there a problem?"

Smiling at her, the man headed around to the rear of her camel, which had now stopped as well. Turning, June watched as he began to unstrap her bag, and she began to realize that the journey seemed now to be over after almost three hours of trekking through the desert. At the same time, when she looked around, she saw nothing but more sand stretching out in every direction, as well as a small rocky outcrop poking up at the bottom of the nearest dune.

"I don't understand," she continued as the man lifted her case down and set it on the sand. "Where -"

Before she could finish, the man barked an order and the camel began to crouch, startling June so much that she once again gripped the reins and almost tumbled straight off.

Laughing, the man reached out and took hold of her wrist, before pulling gently. He said something, a short phrase that he repeated over and over as if he was trying to make her understand; finally June realized that he wanted her to climb off, so she obliged with some degree of awkwardness until she was standing next to the camel, at which point she looked around again.

Pointing past her, the man seemed to be indicating the clump of rocks at the foot of the dune.

"There?" June said cautiously. "I don't understand, I'm supposed to meet Doctor Weaver."

"Weaver," the man replied, pointing again. "Weaver. Weaver."

"There?" June said incredulously. "Doctor

Weaver's down there?"

"Weaver," he said again, nodding this time. "Weaver." He took a step back and briefly crossed his hands against his chest, and now he briefly shook his head.

"So you're not coming any closer?" June said, realizing that despite his smile the man seemed a little nervous.

"Weaver," he repeated, still pointing past the dune.

"I see," she said, understanding at last that she seemed to have reached her destination. "And you're sure about that, are you? I'm sorry, I don't mean to doubt you, it's just that this does all seem rather... random."

"Weaver," he said yet again, pointing toward the bottom of the dune as he began to attach the reins of her camel to the harness of his own, before climbing up onto the camel he'd been riding.

"Okay, then," June replied, glancing at the rocks again and this time spotting movement as a figure rose up as if from some hidden spot behind the rocks. She squinted, watching the figure, but at least this sign of life gave her hope that she wasn't merely being deposited alone in the middle of the desert. "Well, I suppose I should thank you. I'm not _"

The camel let out another grunt, and she turned to see that the shepherd was leading the two beasts back the way they'd just come.

"Thank you!" she called out. "Thank you very much, you've been most kind. Did... did someone arrange for you to pick me up again in a day or two?" She waited, but the shepherd offered no reply. "Did someone do that?" she shouted. "Hello? Do you know when you're supposed to come and collect me?"

The camels stopped and the shepherd turned to her. Silhouetted against the blinding sun, he paused for a moment before pointing at the camel June had been riding.

"Maggie Thatcher!" he yelled, before laughing hysterically and tapping the other camel's flank, then setting off again across the sand.

As she stood with her suitcase all alone at the top of the dune, Sister June could still hear the man laughing to himself as he led his camels away.

***

Stumbling a little as she reached the bottom of the dune, Sister June almost lost her footing but at the last moment she somehow managed to stay upright. Clutching her suitcase, she looked over her shoulder for a moment and saw that a gentle wind was already blowing away all sign of her footsteps.

"Hey!" a woman's voice shouted suddenly. "Over here!"

Turning, June saw that the figure on the rocks was now waving at her. The scene was somewhat surreal, as if the woman had simply popped up out of nowhere, and June took a moment to regather her composure before starting to make her way over. She still found it hard going on the sand, but finally she reached the edge of the rocks just as the woman clambered down to join her.

"Wow," the woman said, lifting her sunglasses briefly to get a better look, "when they said to expect a nun, they weren't kidding. I kind of assumed that was a typo."

"My name -"

"June something," the woman continued, reaching out and forcibly shaking her hand. "Yeah, I paid attention. My name's Stella."

"I'm here to see -"

"Doctor Weaver," she said. "I know. He's my father."

"Ah," June replied, feeling a little more comfortable now she knew with absolute certainty that she was at least in the right place. "That's good. I wasn't entirely sure."

"Were you worried you'd have to hail a passing camel for another ride?"

"Is that how it works here?"

"Uh, sure," Stella replied, furrowing her brow for a moment before setting her sunglasses back into place. "I hope you won't take this the wrong way, Sister June, but I get the feeling that you're something of a duck out of water in a place like this."

"I -"

"A penguin in the desert, one might say."

"I suppose that's one way of looking at it," June said a little stiffly. "I'm terribly sorry, you'll have to forgive me but I wasn't given very much information before I came out here, so I'm not entirely sure what's going on."

"Is that so?"

"I barely even know where I am."

"You really *are* a fish out of water," Stella said, looking her up and down before reaching over and taking the suitcase from her hands. "Come on, I'll carry this," she added, before turning and climbing back over the rocks. "You'll have to forgive the rough terrain, I'm afraid we don't offer much in the way of a butler service out here, but I'll do my best. We don't get many visitors so my hostess skills are a little rusty."

"Indeed," June said, hurrying after her, having to drop onto all fours for a moment as she clambered across the rocks. "I'm so terribly sorry, you're going to think that I'm awfully ignorant, but I'm not sure that this is quite what I was expecting. I've never been to the desert before, at least not to a proper one like this, and I'm starting to think that I'm a little under-prepared."

As she reached the crest of the rocks, she saw that at least there were a couple of small tents on the other side, sheltered from the worst of the sun. She began to make her way down, following the path Stella had taken until she reached the younger woman, who'd set the suitcase on a fold-out table.

"I was sent to see Doctor Mortimer Weaver," she explained, sounding a little out of breath now. "Do you know where I might find him?"

"Of course I know where you might find him," Stella replied with a faint smile, before turning and pointing down into a large hole in the ground. "He's down there."

CHAPTER TWO

"BE CAREFUL," STELLA SAID a couple of minutes later, as she climbed down the rickety ladder that led into the darkness of the hole, "you don't want to trip on your habit."

"Thank you," June replied, taking care to avoid doing just that as she too began to climb down. "I shall do my best."

"That's not a very practical outfit, if you don't mind me pointing out the obvious," Stella continued. "This is probably a silly question, but is there some kind of rule that says you can't take it off? Do you have to wear it even when it's totally wrong for your surroundings?"

"I'm free to make my own judgment," June explained, wincing as the ladder briefly shook. "In this case I deemed it to be most appropriate."

"It's strange hearing another English accent after being out here for so long," Stella told her. "I make a monthly trip into the nearest town, probably the same town you came through. There aren't many English people around, though, so it's nice to hear someone who sounds vaguely familiar. Sorry if that comes across wrong, but I'm sure you know what I mean. It can get rather lonely out here."

"I'm sure your father is good company."

"Have you met him before?"

"I haven't had the pleasure. I've read a few things about him, but I haven't actually met him myself."

"Lucky you," Stella said, stepping off the ladder and then waiting for June to join her. "As his long-suffering daughter, let me tell you that you're in for a treat."

Reaching the bottom of the ladder, June looked up and saw the desert sky high above. Turning, she saw only darkness all around, although after a moment the beam from a flashlight almost blinded her.

"Sorry," Stella said, lowering the beam and then pressing the flashlight itself into June's right hand. "Where *are* my manners?"

June mustered a faint, polite smile as Stella

switched on a second flashlight. Looking past the woman, June saw that they were standing in what appeared to be some kind of cave, with a single long passage leading away into the darkness deep beneath the desert. She adjusted her grip on the flashlight and shone its beam of light along the passage, but all she saw were the rocky walls.

"Yeah, it's not very inviting, is it?" Stella said with a sigh. "Believe me, it doesn't get much better even once you're used to it."

"I'm surprised by how cold it is down here," June said, pulling her shawl away. "Not cold, exactly, more... rather cool."

"You're away from the glare of the desert sun," Stella pointed out. "Even up top, it can get pretty cold at night. Trust me, if you're new to deserts, there are a whole lot of other little surprises waiting for you. I've traveled extensively with Dad, and from jungles to arctic plateaus, this is probably the most inhospitable place I've ever stayed. It can be dangerous, too, if you don't know what you're doing." She paused, before reaching out and patting the side of June's arm. "Don't look so worried, though," she added with a grin. "I'm here to look after you!"

***

"Mind your head," Stella said, not for the first time, as she ducked down and slipped through a narrow part of the dark passageway. "It gets really low for a few meters here, Sister."

"Yes, I see," June said, having to almost bend over double as she turned sideways and maneuvered herself through what was really little more than a crack between two sections of rock.

"Dad thinks there's probably an easier way to get down here," Stella continued, her voice sounding a little leaner now, as if it was bouncing less off the rocky walls of such a cold, confined space. "Not that he's bothered to look for it, of course. Dad's never too fussed about pesky little things like convenience or comfort. He leaves that sort of thing to me."

"And your father's down here at the moment, is he?"

"I'm not sure where else he'd be," Stella pointed out. "As you might have noticed up there, this isn't a great place for a game of hide and seek. And despite the cramped conditions down here, there aren't many nooks and crannies." She was able to stand up a little better as they reached the next section of the passage. "Don't worry, Sister, we're very nearly there."

"I must admit," June said, "this wasn't quite what I expected when I was told – with very little notice – that I was being assigned to the desert. Then again, I really don't know how I was suppose to prepare myself. One doesn't really know where to turn for advice, does one?"

Realizing that Stella had stopped up ahead, June picked her way past the rocks until she reached her, and then she saw that they'd come to an opening in the rock wall. Aiming her flashlight ahead, she saw that the rocks gave way in this area to what appeared to be large, regular blocks that had been used to construct the wall of a much more regular corridor, and there was no doubt in her mind now that what she saw had to be been man-made, albeit probably a very long time in the past.

"And this," Stella said, with a hint of awe in her voice, "is what this whole drama is all about. This is what Dad discovered. Well, with a little help from me, but I'm really not used to getting any credit."

Stepping forward, June reached out and touched the wall, which turned out to feel surprisingly smooth. For a moment, she simply couldn't understand how something so simple could have ended up buried in the rocks far beneath the Saharan desert. She remembered some scraps of information she'd been given over the phone back at the convent – something about an important discovery and some relics – but her mind was racing and she found herself struggling to understand why she of all people would ever be dispatched to such a place.

"What is this?" she asked finally, turning to Stella again.

"Officially?" Pausing for a moment, Stella seemed amused by June's confusion. "Officially it's a site of possible archaeological interest, being worked on below the radar by a lunatic because everyone's worried that different local factions will try to claim the site."

"And unofficially?"

"Unofficially, it might be the most important discovery in the history of mankind," Stella continued, and now her smile had faded, "and believe me, I'm not someone who uses her words loosely."

"We're out in the middle of nowhere," June pointed out.

"Some nowheres used to be somewhere once."

"But -"

"I don't have all the answers," Stella added, interrupting her, "and despite his bluster, my father doesn't either. We're at the very beginning of what might yet turn out to be an immense find, one that fundamentally changes our understanding of human history."

"That sounds... important," June suggested.

"It's more than just important," Stella told her. "I've got to admit, when Dad started explaining his crackpot theories to me, I thought he'd gone off the deep end. I've been waiting for that to happen for most of my life. But the more he told me, and the more evidence he showed me, and the more I looked at that evidence for myself... I don't know, I want to dismiss it, but I just can't."

Hearing a banging sound, June turned to look ahead just as she heard a yelp of pain.

"That's Dad," Stella said with a sigh. "Don't worry, he's probably just smacked his hand with a hammer again. He does things like that." She checked her watch. "In fact, I think I might head back up and check on a few things. Call me crazy, but something tells me that you'll get to know him better if I'm not there to interrupt." She turned to walk away. "I could warn you about a few things, Sister June, but I think I'm going to let you find out for yourself. Good luck, and I mean that. You're gonna need it!"

"Wait!" June called out. "Why did you say

just now that you *want* to dismiss this?"

Stella stopped and glanced back at her.

"Surely if this is as big a find as you intimated," June continued, "it'd make your career. Shouldn't you be excited?"

"I should," Stella added, with a hint of fear in her eyes as the voice yelped again in the distance, "but in this case, I really don't think I like the implications of what my father has found. Because if he's right, nothing on this planet is ever going to be the same again."

CHAPTER THREE

"DAMN IT," THE MAN said as he brushed some more dust from the wall, taking particular care to remove some tiny lumps from the center of a deep crack. "When will I ever learn?"

"Doctor Weaver?"

Startled, the man – short and stocky, with a rough beard – turned to her, and from his expression June could immediately tell that he'd had no idea about her arrival.

"I'm sorry to disturb you," she said, stepping into the small chamber and looking around, immediately spotting strange carvings of what appeared to be unusual letters and words on the walls. "Your daughter showed me down here."

"Who are you?" Weaver asked.

"My name is Sister June."

"You're a nun!"

"I am, and -"

"What's a nun doing in the desert?" he spluttered. "I've never seen a nun in the desert before! Nuns don't turn up in the desert, at least not in my experience!"

"I would imagine there might have been one or two who got lost in the past," she replied, "but I must admit that I probably seem like an unusual sight right now. I've been sent from England by an organization called the First Order that has taken an interest in your work."

"The First Order?" he replied, furrowing his brow. "I've never heard of them."

"I'm not certain," she continued, "but if I had to hazard a guess, I'd say that they probably intercepted some communication you sent at some point recently. Did you, perhaps, contact anyone else?"

"I sent a telegram to my office at the university," he said cautiously. "That's all."

"Then the First Order evidently go to that telegram first."

"That's impossible," he told her. "I sent it explicitly to my colleague Doctor Dernier and I made sure that it wasn't to be opened by anyone else. How could this First Order get hold of it?"

"They have their ways," June said as she made her way across the empty chamber and looked at some more of the lettering. "Let me assure you that I'm only here to help. To observe, really. The First Order want me to find out exactly what you've got here and report back to them."

"Why?"

"I suppose they're curious."

"Why?"

"They take an interest in such things."

"Why?"

"I'm afraid I really don't know, to be honest," she said, stopping next to him and looking at some more of the carvings. "I've never been about to find out. Do you know what these are? What language are they written in?"

"You can't just come in here and start demanding answers!" he said firmly. "Give me one good reason why I should tell you a damn thing!"

She turned to him.

"Excuse the language," he added, "although I should warn you, I know some much worse words and I *will* use them if I think they're appropriate."

"The First Order sends me to investigate certain unusual phenomena," she explained, although she supposed that this wasn't quite the time to start mentioning bears and mermaids and vampires. "I really don't know the full extent of their interest, I suppose they don't think that it's much of my business, but the point is that they like me to go around the world compiling little reports for them."

She waited for a reply, but now she could tell that Weaver was not only uncomfortable; he seemed downright suspicious and she had to admit that he had every good reason to feel that way."

"So you seem to have found some kind of hidden chamber deep beneath the desert," she continued, "far away from any other sign of civilization. I can assure you that anything you tell me will be treated in the strictest confidence. If it makes you feel any better, I wasn't exactly *asked* whether I wanted to come here. I was sent my plane tickets and a brief explanation, and otherwise I'm rather in the dark. I didn't bother arguing, because I know from experience that arguing would have done no good."

"So you're saying you were forced to come here?" he replied, raising a skeptical eyebrow. "Why would that make me feel any better?"

"Because it might mean that I'm entirely on your side," she pointed out. "And the sooner you let me know what's going on here, the sooner I might be able to get out of your hair."

***

"The text is like nothing I've seen before," Weaver said a few minutes later, as he led June through a narrow doorway into a second, slightly larger chamber. He shone his flashlight around. "As far as I can tell, it's not really related to any other language groups either."

"What does that mean?"

"It means it seems to have sprung up in a bubble," he continued, stopping to look around. "Nothing influenced its development, and in turn it didn't influence anything else."

"Is that unusual?"

"It's not completely unprecedented," he explained, "but it's odd. Then again, nothing about this place makes a whole lot of sense."

June looked at a large stone altar in the middle of the chamber, although she realized after a moment that it might not be an altar at all. Making her way over, she brushed some dust from the surface and saw that here too there was lots of the strange writing.

"It's a tomb," Weaver said.

She turned to him.

"There's a body in there," he continued. "At least, I'm pretty sure there is. There are certainly no signs of grave-robbing."

"How can you be sure that it's a tomb?"

"Experience, mainly. Gut instinct." He stepped over to the tomb's other side and looked down at the top section." This part here moves aside," he explained. "Every time I've ever seen anything remotely like this, it's always turned out to be a tomb of some kind. My best guess right now is that when I get this thing open, I'm going to find some kind of ancient ruler who was put in here back in the day."

"How old do you think it is?"

"I've been having trouble placing it, but based on a few preliminary observations, I'd guess it's from anywhere between five and ten thousand years ago."

"And it has been down here, untouched and ignored, for all that time?"

"What's wrong?" he asked with a faint smile. "Does that thought give you the creeps?"

"Not exactly," she replied, "although I must admit that, in my line of work, I tend not to look too favorably on the concept of grave-robbing." She looked past him and saw another doorway, leading into what appeared to be darkness. "What's through there?"

"Are you sure you want to know?" he said, before gesturing for her to follow as he made his way over to the far corner and looked through into the void. "Steps," he explained as she headed over to join him. "Leading further down."

"Down to where?"

"Patience, Sister June," he said with a sigh. "I've had a little look, but I've really only scratched the surface. To be honest, at first I couldn't get my head around any of it, because the basic features of the architecture made no sense until I learned to look at it from a different perspective."

"What perspective is that?"

"How did you get in here?"

"Your daughter showed me the entrance."

"Stella's a good girl," he replied, "and she's too smart to make such a rudimentary mistake. There's no way she would have described that hole in the ground as the entrance."

"I suppose she didn't," June admitted. "So where *is* the entrance?"

"That's something I've yet to work out," he said, as he shone his flashlight through the doorway, illuminating a set of stone steps running steeply down deeper into the ground. "This complex is much larger than I originally thought, and I haven't even scratched the surface with my exploration so far."

"Well, I..."

June's words trailed off for a moment as she tried to understand exactly what he meant. Still looking down the stairs, she tried to understand exactly what he meant, yet somehow she felt as if nothing quite made sense.

"Still," Weaver continued, "you've arrived at a very opportune moment. In fact, I'd argue that you couldn't have timed things any better."

"And why's that?" June asked, still looking down the steps that led further into the underground darkness.

"Because after all my preparatory work, today's the big day," Weaver said as she turned to him. He smiled, and then he nodded toward the sarcophagus in the middle of the chamber. "Today's the day when I open this thing and take a look at whoever or whatever's inside."

CHAPTER FOUR

"YOU'RE CRAZY," STELLA SAID as she set some oily rags down on one of the makeshift tables in the tent above ground. "You're not remotely equipped to do something like this. You realize that, don't you?"

"I've got a crowbar," Weaver pointed out with a smile. "What more do I need?"

"You're going to open that sarcophagus with a crowbar?" she replied, clearly horrified by the suggestion.

"I've exhausted all the other possibilities," he told her, "and besides, the sarcophagus itself isn't of any interest. It's rectangular and it doesn't feature any decorative flourishes. I'm far more interested in finding out what's inside."

"So you think that justifies acting as a

barbarian?" Stella snapped, picking up a spanner before slamming it back down and turning to her father. "This type of work needs to be conducted slowly and carefully over many months. If you were thinking straight, you'd be calling in outside help rather than blundering along like this."

"How did I raise such a scaredy-cat?" Weaver asked, before chuckling. "Then again, I suppose this part of your personality's more down to your mother."

"Don't bring her into this!" Stella hissed.

"She never understood my pioneering spirit," Weaver continued. "She was like you, she thought every little step had to be documented and tested in advance. I'm going to tell you exactly what I told her all those years ago. Sometimes, my girl, you just have to push on ahead and take a few risks. Isn't that right, Sister?"

He stared at his daughter for a few more seconds, before turning to see that June was still sitting obediently on her little fold-out chair in the corner.

"Well," June said after a moment, feeling a little lost for words, "I mean... I... I have no experience in this field, but -"

"But you understand my point, right?" Weaver continued. "When a man's faced with the opportunity of a lifetime, he can't just pussy-foot around at the edge. He has to dive right in!"

"I can see the benefit of getting on with things," June said cautiously, fully aware that Stella seemed to be on the verge of boiling over with rage, "although sometimes it's wise to be a little more careful. I suppose really it all depends on the situation at hand."

"Well, it's my expedition," Weaver said, shaking his head, "and that means that I get to decide. And I've decided that this afternoon I'll be opening that sarcophagus down there, and then we'll see what we've got our hands on." He stepped past his daughter and made his way out of the tent. "No man ever achieved greatness by holding back and doing things by the book."

Once Weaver was gone, June felt as if she should say something to try to make Stella feel better, although as the silence persisted she realized that she might just make things worse.

"He's insane," Stella said finally, leaning against the table with her back to June. "He's blundering on, trying to prove something, and he might very well wreck one of the world's most fascinating archaeological discoveries."

"I'm sure he knows what he's doing," June suggested.

"Are you?" Stella asked, turning to her. "With all due respect, you don't know how these things work. A site like this should take years to explore, but Dad's charging around like he has to get the whole thing done in a matter of days. He hasn't even mapped it out fully, he hasn't even found the entrance yet or begun to translate the inscriptions, and already he wants to crack open that thing down there."

"Is that really such a bad idea?" June asked.

"Yes!" she snapped, before letting out a heavy sigh. "The damage he could cause to an irreplaceable historical site is incalculable. The rules about this sort of thing exist for a reason."

"I don't doubt you for one moment," June told her. "But if your father is determined to break those rules, then there must surely be a good reason."

***

"Now where's that ether cylinder," Weaver muttered under his breath, crouching in front of the large trunk of tools out past the side of the tent. "I know I saw that damn thing yesterday!"

"Mr. Weaver," June said, having made her way out of the tent to find him, "I wonder, might I have a word?"

"If you're trying to stop me," he replied, "then save your breath. I'm sorry, I don't mean to be rude, but this job isn't going to wait."

"Hasn't it already waited many thousands of years?"

"Damn it, you've been listening to my daughter, haven't you?" he murmured, not even turning to look at her as he continued to sort through the tools. "You'd think it should be the other way round, wouldn't you? You'd think that she'd be the impatient one and I'd be the voice of reason."

"I'm sure you both have your points of view," June continued, "and I'm sure you can both justify those points, but -"

"Is this a nun thing?"

"I beg your pardon?"

"Do you have some kind of obligation to always be diplomatic?" he asked, finally turning to look at her. He raised a hand to shield his eyes from the glare of the desert sun. "If so, you should be aware that it's verging on being annoying."

"I -"

"Because you don't know anything about this line of work," he added, "and frankly, Stella's only just started out in the field herself. I, meanwhile, have been a working archaeologist for thirty years, and I think I've earned the right to a little respect."

"Of course," she told him, "but -"

"So do you have any idea how exhausting it is to be questioned all the time?" he asked. "To be doubted? I wouldn't come into your church and start telling you what to do on your own altar, so why do you think you should be telling me how to go about this project? And Stella, bless her, has read all the books in the world but she doesn't have much experience getting her hands dirty." He paused for a moment. "That's the problem these days, you've got all these people running around trying to poke their noses in, and all they're really doing is getting in the way of the people who know how things work."

"Is there perhaps a middle ground?" June asked. "Could you compromise?"

"Compromise is for wimps," he replied, before wincing as he got to his feet. "As I understand it, Sister June, you're here as an observer, so I've got one word of advice for you." He pointed at her. "Observe!"

"If -"

"And the best way to observe is to keep your trap shut!" he added. "Just observe and -"

Before he could finish, he broke into a heavy coughing fit. Reaching into his pocket, he pulled out a handkerchief and held it against his mouth. The coughing fit continued for several more seconds before he was able to get it under control. Finally he pulled the handkerchief away, and June noticed some spots of blood as he quickly scrunched it up and stuffed it back into his pocket. She opened her mouth to ask him of he was alright, but at the last second she realized that most likely he really wasn't interested in anything she might have to say.

"Just observe and make your notes," he continued, sounding a little breathless now, "and let me get on with what I do best. Because there are some secrets to be learned at this site, and I'm damn well going to learn at least some of them before the bureaucrats and bean-counters and government officials show up and take everything over. They'll get their chance soon enough, I won't keep the site hidden from them forever, and once they arrive everything'll grind to a halt and we'll all be lucky if we're still alive by the time anyone makes any interesting discoveries." He picked up a few tools from the side and carried them past the other end of the tent. "They can have their caution later," he added. "Let me have my speed now."

Again June opened her mouth to say something, but she really wasn't sure what she could possibly contribute.

"He's dying."

Turning, she saw that Stella was in the entrance to the tent, and that she'd evidently been listening to the whole conversation.

"It doesn't take Sherlock Holmes to figure that out," Stella continued with tears in her eyes. "He won't admit it, but he doesn't have long left. So I really can't blame him too much for wanting to get on with things. He wants to see what he's discovered while he still can."

AMY CROSS

CHAPTER FIVE

"WE'RE ALMOST READY," WEAVER said a short while later as he stepped around the sarcophagus in the chamber, holding a crowbar slightly menacingly over his shoulder. "I just need to pick the perfect spot to start."

"Penny for your thoughts?"

Realizing that she'd been staring down the steps into the darkness for a while now, June turned to see that Stella had made her way over.

"Sorry," Stella continued, "I didn't mean to criticize." Now she too looked down the steps. "Sometimes I do the same thing. I just look down there and wonder what else we might be able to discover."

"Have you been down there?" June asked. "Is it safe?"

"I've got no reason to believe that it's *not* safe," Stella told her. "Sure, Dad and I have been down and checked it out. There are more corridors, more sets of stairs, and there are some parts where the roof's come down. It's a real maze, but we haven't found any more chambers."

"Do you think there might be more?"

"I don't know why anyone would have gone to all the trouble of cutting these passages deeper and deeper underground if there weren't," Stella explained. "The amount of work required to create this site must have been phenomenal." She glanced over her shoulder and saw that her father was still examining the sarcophagus, still muttering away to himself. "That's another reason why I'm worried he's putting the cart before the horse. This particular sarcophagus is so close to the surface, that means it's unlikely that the entire tomb structure was built for whoever's in there. He's about to uncover some third or fourth wife, or a servant or a priest, something like that."

"Then who *was* this tomb built for?"

"Someone important," Stella said firmly, turning to her again with a hint of fear in her eyes. "An emperor, perhaps, or at least a king. Or perhaps even someone grander. Whoever they are, however, they'd be much further away from the surface." They both looked down the steps again, into the darkness. "Whoever this tomb was built for, my guess is that they're waiting way down there. Dad knows that too, but for all his talk of bravado, he knows that's an undertaking too far."

"Why?"

"Because he's too sick to go all the way down there," she said, lowering a voice a little so she couldn't be heard. "I don't know exactly what he's got, but he crept off to see some doctors before we left England. Several times, actually. He thinks I don't know. And I'm sure it's not a coincidence that right about that time, he suddenly cut his forty-fag-a-day smoking habit."

"I've found the spot!" Weaver announced grandly.

June and Stella turned to see that he was standing at the far end of the sarcophagus.

"There's a very small pre-existing weakness here," he continued, tapping the stone with the end of the crowbar. "That should make this a little easier, and I don't know about you ladies, but I for one am all for making things easier wherever possible."

"Do you want me to do it, Dad?" Stella asked.

"You?" He chuckled again. "I might be getting old, my dear, but I think I'm still the strongest one in this room." He began to push the crowbar's tip into the crack beneath the lid of the sarcophagus. "The day I'm weaker than a young woman and a nun is the day I really have to consider giving up this line of work."

"Sorry, I forget," Stella whispered, leaning closer to June as her father started jiggling the crowbar, "Dad's a bit of a misogynistic relic. It's the 1980s and he still thinks women can't do anything more physical than make cups of tea for the menfolk."

"He's set in his ways," June suggested with a faint, knowing smile. "Everybody is of their time. Even us."

"It's a little harder to budge than I'd expected," Weaver explained as June made her way over, followed by Stella. "When these people were entombed like this, there was never any expectation that they'd be dug up. Now, there are some silly people who think people like me shouldn't be doing this at all, that we're disrespecting the dead by tampering with their graves. And do you know what I say to those people?"

"What?" June asked.

Stella rolled her eyes.

"I tell them to come and stop me," Weaver continued with a grin. "Stop all the jibber-jabbering and talk, and if you feel so strongly, come and physically try to stop me." He adjusted his position a little before pushing on the crowbar again. "They never do, though," he added through clenched teeth. "They prefer to criticize from the safety of their desks. The idea of coming out into the field and getting their hands dirty is -"

Before he could finish, the top of the sarcophagus suddenly shifted slightly. Caught a little off-guard, Weaver almost fell forward before managing to steady himself, and then he tossed the crowbar aside and grabbed his flashlight. Leaning down, he struggled to peer through the fairly small gap he'd made at the top of the sarcophagus, but after a few more seconds he set the flashlight down on the floor and began to try to push the top section fully out of the way.

"Help me!" he gasped. "Hurry, there's a body in here!"

Stella opened her mouth to reply, but hesitating for a moment and then hurrying over. June hesitated a little longer, not quite sure whether she should assist in the disturbance of a grave, but finally she told herself that this was more of a historical site than a cemetery, so she stepped around the sarcophagus and at least pretended to help push the lid, even if she felt too uncomfortable to offer much help. Gradually the lid began to grind away from its position, and after a couple more minutes it toppled over the other side of the sarcophagus, landing with a heavy thud on the ground and cracking into two pieces.

As Weaver waved dust from the air and shone his flashlight down, the three observers looked into the sarcophagus and gradually began to make out a thin, seemingly mummified figure resting on its back with loose bandages having for the most part fallen away.

June let out a shocked gasp as she saw patches of mottled skin still clinging to bone. When she looked at the figure's head, she saw that its jaw was open, revealing two rows of rotten teeth; the eyes, meanwhile, had shrunk to almost nothing, while a few strands of hair still clung to the scalp.

"Is that..."

Her voice trailed off.

"Whoever this was," Weaver said after a moment, "he must have been important if he was placed down here. He might not have been the owner of the tomb – in fact, I'm sure he wasn't – but he was perhaps an attendant of some kind." He glanced at Stella. "Believe me, I've been fully aware from the start that this was only the start of the exploration process."

"What are those items?" June asked, pointing at various pin-like tools next to the figure's left hand.

Leaning down a little more, Weaver picked one of the items up and examined it more closely; as he turned it around, he saw the sharp, hooked tip.

"Fascinating," he murmured. "This poor fellow was mummified after his death, and evidently the tools were placed in the sarcophagus with him. This, for example, would have been pushed up through the nostrils and forced into the skull, and then the brain would have been scooped out. It's not unlike the methods used by the Ancient Egyptians, although whether there was any contact with that civilization remains to be seen. The process might well have been developed here independently."

"What a horrid ritual," June said cautiously.

"Is it really so bad?" Weaver asked, turning to her. "Don't you lot literally pretend to eat the flesh and blood of your master?"

"Let's not go down that route right now," Stella said, clearly trying to be tactful. "I'm sorry, Sister June, but Dad has never been a big fan of religion." She turned to her father. "But this isn't the time to be having that debate, is it? Because whatever you might believe or not believe, Dad, whoever put this guy down here obviously *did* have some kind of belief, and if we don't respect that, how are we ever going to understand them?"

Weaver muttered something under his breath, but June could tell that he wasn't entirely in agreement.

"So now what?" she asked, as she looked down once more at the mummified figure in the sarcophagus and felt a shiver run through her bones. "Exactly how are you going to proceed?"

"With caution," Weaver said, as he set the

needle-like object back in its place. "But one way or another, I'm going to find a way to make this fellow give up *all* his secrets."

CHAPTER SIX

"I'VE NEVER SEEN ANYTHING quite like it," Weaver muttered a couple of hours later, as he continued to examine the figure in the sarcophagus. "Do you see these small dark piles of powder, Stella? Based on my experience, if these are the types of herbs that I think they are, I might have to revise my estimates as to when this body was put in here."

"Revise them in which direction?" Stella asked.

"I think this place is older than I ever dreamed possible," he explained. "We'll need to run some proper tests back at home, but this site might be ten thousand years old."

"No way," Stella replied. "That would put it before Mesopotamia."

"I'm well aware of the implications, thank you," he said firmly.

"So there has to be a mistake," she pointed out. "The area above this tomb -"

"We still haven't found the entrance," he continued, interrupting her. "I'm rather tired of you pointing out the obvious all the time. Once we find the entrance, we'll have a much easier time analyzing its relationship to the surface area, and that will allow us to produce a more accurate guess." He leaned a little further into the sarcophagus. "We're still gathering information. Let's not lose sight of that fact."

As Stella continued to pepper her father with questions, June was sitting on the floor in the far corner, scribbling some observations in her notebook. She'd written down the facts as she understood them, and now she'd begun to try to sketch out the scene to the best of her abilities; she'd never considered herself to be much of an artist, but so far she was managing to produce a reasonable impression of the chamber, and she supposed that this would be more than enough to convey a sense of the place to her superiors at the First Order.

Focusing on adding some shade to the bottom of the sketch, she was barely aware now of Weaver and his daughter still talking. After a few more seconds, however, she heard a faint shuffling sound and looked to her left.

All she saw was the open doorway that led down to the steps.

The shuffling sound had stopped now, and June told herself that she'd probably been imagining things. Returning her attention to the notebook, she used her pencil to add a little more texture to the drawing of the sarcophagus, but almost immediately she began to hear the shuffling sound again.

She instinctively looked back over at the doorway. Already the sound had faded, but June couldn't help wondering whether there might be something down there. She thought of the steps leading deep into the darkness, and she knew that she'd get short shrift from Weaver if she dared to suggest that she'd heard anything at all. She watched the doorway for a few more seconds, just long enough to calm her fears, and then she turned back to her sketch.

"June," a man's voice whispered.

Startled, she turned and looked at the doorway again. She felt her heart pounding in her chest as she stared, but when she looked over at Weaver and Stella she saw that they were still deep in discussion; evidently they hadn't heard the voice, so after a few seconds she got to her feet and made her way across the chamber. Stopping at the doorway, she looked down the steps and saw only darkness below.

She waited, but now all she heard was the

muffled voices of Weaver and Stella coming from over her shoulder. A moment later she turned to walk away, but at the last second she heard the voice again.

"June."

Looking down the steps again, she realized now that she felt drawn to go and take a closer look. She knew that was a foolish idea, of course, yet somehow she felt almost as if an invisible force was trying to encourage her to investigate; replaying the voice over and over in her mind, she knew that it wasn't familiar at all, that it had sounded old and dark and cracked, but the more she stared at the darkness – and the more she tried to resist – the more she felt as if in some way the darkness at the foot of the steps was staring straight back at her, and the owner of the voice was waiting just out of sight.

Finally, almost involuntarily, she took a step down, and then another. She could feel the air getting colder already, and she had to reach out to steady herself against the rocky wall, but soon she took a third step, then a fourth, and now she felt as if the answer to all her questions must surely be waiting just out of sight, just beyond the darkness, just at the foot of the steps and -

"Sister June?"

Letting out a startled cry, she spun around and almost lost her footing. The notebook and pencil fell from her hands, and then she sighed as she found herself staring up at Stella.

"Sister June, are you okay?" Stella asked. "You seemed to be in a world of your own."

"I'm perfectly fine," June replied, feeling utterly idiotic now and wondering why she ever contemplated going down the steps. In fact, she felt almost as if she'd been in a trance. "I was just... taking a look, that's all."

"I was calling you over to see if you wanted to see what Dad's up to," Stella explained. "I said your name three or four times."

"I just got lots in my thoughts for a second or two," June said, starting to follow Stella up before realizing that she'd misplaced her notebook. Remembering that it had fallen from her hand, she looked back down and saw it resting on one of the other steps. "Just one moment."

Hurrying down, she picked the notebook and pencil up. As she did so, she glanced further into the darkness, and for a moment she was struck once again by the sense that the darkness was almost waiting for her. She knew she should simply turn and go back up, of course, yet she felt herself once more being drawn deeper and deeper beneath the surface, to the extent that she only just managed to stop herself following the steps further down.

"That's quite enough of that," she told herself as she turned and began to make her way back up.

Once she was near the top, she saw that Stella had stopped to examine some strange lettering that had been carved long ago into the doorway, facing away from the chamber and down toward the bottom of the steps. Looking more closely at the lettering, June could tell that it was in the same language as the inscriptions in the rest of the tomb, although she had absolutely no idea what any of it meant.

"You know," Stella said after a moment, "this is going to sound nuts, and I'd never admit it to Dad, but there are times when..."

Reaching out, she began to trace some of the markings.

"There are times," she continued cautiously, "when I almost feel like I understand this."

"You do?"

"And yet I also don't," Stella added. "I'm not even explaining myself very well, but it's as if even though this text seems like gobbledygook, on some deeper level some part of it seems familiar."

"Have you perhaps seen something similar somewhere before?"

"It's not like that," Stella said. "It's more like... I'm missing something obvious. It's like I'm not seeing something that's right in front of my face."

"Would it be alright if I took a rubbing?" June asked.

"For your personal curiosity?"

"Something like that," June replied, tearing a sheet of paper from her notebook and placing it against some of the text, before making marks on the paper with her pencil, causing the outline of the lettering to show through. "Don't worry," she added, "I won't go around showing it to people willy-nilly."

"Not even your First Order friends?"

"They'll be discrete," June insisted. "They're *always* discrete, that's kind of their whole reason for being."

"At this point," Stella replied, "I'll take any help we can get." She watched as June finished. "I feel like, when I finally understand this language, I'm going to feel so stupid for not getting it before. Dad thinks this whole place might have developed with no interference from the outside world, at a time when there wasn't really much of an outside world at all, but I'm really not so sure. Something about this whole place just doesn't add up. It's almost like it's all upside-down and inside-out and screwy."

"I read up on you and your father before I came here," June admitted. "You're both very well-known in your areas of expertise."

"That isn't helping much right now," Stella muttered, sounding as if she was close to defeat as she once again reached out and touched the markings on the wall. "Right now, I feel like I've got no idea what I'm doing at all."

CHAPTER SEVEN

STANDING A LITTLE WAY past the tent, June watched as the sun continued to set in the distance. Now that darkness was falling, the desert seemed completely different; stars were visible in the night sky, but the desert itself was a vast arena of nothingness, and June felt a shiver pass through her bones as she realized that she was so very far from civilization.

She also felt a little nippy, since the temperature had dropped considerably.

"First time?"

Turning, she saw that Doctor Weaver had made his way over.

"In the desert, I mean," he continued. "Especially at night. It can be a spooky place, huh?"

"I'm okay with spooky," she told him. "I've

done spooky before. I must admit, however, that I feel strange being so far from the nearest town or village. I suppose I shouldn't react in that manner, yet I can't help myself."

"It can get cold out here," he replied. "That's something people don't really expect with the desert, but once the sun sets any heat in the sand quickly radiates into the air, and until morning there's no more sunlight to reheat it, so the temperature can really plummet. And then, come the morning, the sun'll come up and the temperature'll soar again." He looked at the steaming cup in her hands. "You've got the right idea, though," he added. "There's nothing like a nice cup of tea in the Sahara."

"You're right," she told him. "I've never been anywhere like this before. I feel very much like the proverbial fish out of water."

"I imagine you nuns lead quite the cloistered life," he replied. "Pardon the pun."

"I've traveled more than you might think," she said as she looked out across the desert again, "but certainly this feels as strange and as alien as anywhere else. Then again, one must always be open to new experiences, so I shall take this opportunity to take in the wonder of another part of the Lord's creation."

"Is it that easy?"

"I don't know what you mean."

"I mean that you could use that argument in any situation, but it might not necessarily have much meaning. Do you look for the wonder of the Lord's creation when you see a child dying of a curable disease? Do you see it when you hear of the atrocities mankind commits?"

"I have my faith."

"And that's enough?"

"Faith gets me through even the most difficult of moments," she told him. "I understand only too well that it's not for us to try to explain the Lord's choices. We must simply do the best that we can, in the situations in which we find ourselves, and hope that we are contributing in some small way to the betterment of life for others."

"I've not heard it put quite like that before," he admitted. "And this First Order organization sounds a little -"

Before he could finish, he broke into a coughing fit. As the fit continued, he leaned against the side of the tent, and June reached over and patted him gently on the back; still the fit refused to pass, and June began to worry as Weaver bent forward as if he might be about to collapse.

"I'm fine!" he spluttered, clearly struggling to get himself back under control. "Just give me a moment."

Sure enough, after a few more seconds he began to pull himself together, although his first impulse was to look back toward the tent as if he was worried he might have disturbed his daughter.

"She's asleep," he said breathlessly, before turning to June. "Everything's alright, there's no need to worry. Please, don't mention this to Stella." He wiped some specks of blood from his lips. "I just need to figure out what I've found here so that I can hand the whole project over to her. She's such a good archaeologist, she needs her big break. And that's exactly what this discovery is going to become."

***

Several hours later, flat on her back on a makeshift bed in one corner of the tent, June stared up at the canvas and listened to the silence all around. She'd slept in some unusual places over the years, but somehow she felt particularly discomforted by the idea of being in the desert with nothing but miles of sand stretching to the horizon in every direction.

"I really don't think that I'm the right person for this particular assignment," she remembered telling the voice on the phone. "Aren't there *any* other people who might -"

"This assignment has been given to you," the voice had said firmly, interrupting her. "Your tickets have been arranged and you'll leave in the morning."

"But, I thought perhaps I wouldn't have to do this again."

"Why would you think that?"

In truth, after her visit to New York, she'd hoped that she was finally free from the First Order. After all, eleven happy years had passed since those strange events, eleven years in which she'd gradually come to believe that maybe – just maybe – the phone wasn't about to ring with another absurd mission. She'd spent that time working at the convent, getting on with her daily chores and letting all thoughts of her adventures slip into the past. She'd even been left untroubled by John, and although she hoped that he was out there somewhere getting on with his life, she had to admit that she'd been glad to think her own roving days were over. She'd finally come to believe that she would never again have to leave the convent, and that thought had made her so happy.

And then, one morning a week earlier, the phone had rung and the First Order had pushed its way back into her life.

"I don't know why I thought it," she remembered telling the man on the phone. "I've just been so busy here, and I do feel it's worth pointing out that I'm not exactly a spring chicken these days. I was still fairly young when I went to New York, I was in my thirties, and now I'm forty-six and -"

"All these factors have been taken into

consideration," the voice had said, cutting her off yet again.

"I'm sure they have," she'd continued, trying to think of some other excuse that might make the First Order think again. "I don't know if you're aware," she'd added, "but next week is St. Jude's annual chrysanthemum competition and I'm expected to run the tombola, which might not sound like much but it actually requires a great deal of preparation. In fact, I was just thinking last night that I should get on with that, because time is getting on and the visitors tend to complain if they're not happy with the prizes. One of the main problems with a tombola at a flower competition is that one has to try to determine whether to keep the prizes strictly related to horticulture, or whether one wants to branch out and – if so – in what direction. If you've never organized a tombola at a chrysanthemum competition before, then let me tell you, the politics can be extreme."

She'd waited, wondering whether she might have managed to wriggle out of the assignment.

"Your tickets," the voice had replied finally, sounding distinctly unimpressed, "will be waiting for you at the counter at the airport. The procedure for picking them up will be the same as usual."

June had sighed, and that had been the moment when she'd realized that there was no escaping the tendrils of the First Order. And now, as a gentle gust of wind blew against the side of the tent, she felt a shiver run through her bones as the chilly night reminded her – not that she needed reminding – that she was so very far from home. She could only hope that young Sister Monica would be able to navigate the politics of the chrysanthemum show and would manage not to annoy Mrs. Moorgate, who tended to be -

Suddenly hearing a bumping sound coming from outside the tent, June sat up. With moonlight picking out the tent's canvas, she looked over and saw that Weaver and his daughter were still fast asleep, but a moment later she heard the bump again and she realized with a fright that something or somebody was definitely outside. She opened her mouth to call out to the others and wake them, but at the last second she reminded herself that she had a certain degree of experience when it came to dealing with the unexplained. A fraction of a second later she heard the bumping sound for a third time, and she swallowed hard as she realized that a little discretion and diplomacy might in fact be the order of the day.

AMY CROSS

CHAPTER EIGHT

AS SOON AS SHE'D opened the flap at the front of the tent, June realized she could hear the sound of somebody shuffling about on the far side of the small camp. She stopped for a moment, wondering whether some passing shepherd might have chanced upon the site, but somehow deep down she felt certain that this was unlikely; her mind's eye returned to the poor mummified man in the sarcophagus, but she felt that this too was probably not a realistic explanation.

A moment later she heard the distinctive sound of somebody knocking one of the saucepans over by the campfire.

Stepping around past the side of the tent, she resolved to approach the intruder with caution. She had no weapon with her, but she told herself that she needed no such thing; she'd faced all sorts of creatures over the years while working for the First Order, and she'd come to believe that she was well equipped to deal with anything that might be thrown her way. As she reached the other end of the tent she stopped and squinted as she look toward the other side of the camp, and sure enough she spotted something crawling past the fold-out seats that Weaver had set up earlier. Whatever was at the camp, it was clearly human, even if it was moving on all fours.

June thought for a moment, and then she took another step forward.

"Hello?" she called out. "There's no need to be afraid, I'm only trying to see whether you need -"

As soon as those words left her lips, she heard a loud clattering sound. A flash of movement moved past the other end of the camp and quickly disappeared down into the hole in the ground, and a moment later June heard a loud thud as if something had dropped down into the tomb itself.

"Wait!" she shouted, hurrying over to the hole and looking down. "There's really no need to run, I'm only trying to help you. Are you from round here?"

She waited, but the only sound she heard – a moment later – was a shuffling sound coming from somewhere over her shoulder.

"Sister June?" Weaver said, sounding a little

sleepy and rather grumpy. "What's going on out here?"

She turned to him and saw that Stella was a few steps back.

"Was it a scorpion?" Weaver continued. "Christ, woman, it's the middle of the night! What are you doing running around in the camp?"

***

"There's no-one for miles and miles around," Weaver muttered under his breath as he stepped into the chamber and shone his flashlight past the sarcophagus. "There's obviously no sign of a disturbance in here!"

"I know what I saw," June replied, her heart still racing as she shone her own flashlight across the room.

"I really don't think you do."

"I'm not prone to imagining things!"

"Sister, please," he continued, turning to her with a sigh, "just think about it for a moment. You're a nun in the desert, you're completely out of your comfort zone, it's obvious that you had a bad dream and when you woke up you had a little trouble telling reality from fantasy."

"Those pots and pans were knocked over," she pointed out.

"You probably bumped them."

"I was nowhere near them."

"There's wind out here in the desert," he continued. "You must have noticed, there are gusts all the time. If one of those gusts coincided with... with some kind of unusual shadow, it's entirely possible that your were disorientated. Hell, it's fairly likely, given the circumstances."

"I might be a nun," she replied, choosing her word with care, "but I can assure you that I've got quite a lot of experience in the world. I've... been around."

"Around the convent?" he suggested with a hint of disdain.

"America," she replied, trying to avoid sounding too irritated. "Switzerland." She thought for a moment, aware that she'd really run out of examples. "Cornwall."

"Well, there's no-one here now."

June hesitated, before making her way to the sarcophagus and shining her flashlight's beam inside. She half-expected now to find that the mummified body had shifted, or that it was entirely missing, but to her relief she saw that it was in exactly the same spot as before.

"Are you scared of the mummy?" Weaver asked.

June turned to him.

"Been watching too many horror films, have we?" he continued.

"I don't think this is helping," Stella said, sounding particularly exhausted. "There's obviously no-one here now, but I suppose it's possible that some local wildlife entered the camp. Sister June, is it possible that what you saw might have been a lizard of some kind? Or a small dog?"

"It was a person."

"But you said it was on its hands and knees."

"I know what I said," she replied, before realizing that she perhaps sounded a little too defensive. "It wasn't a lizard and it wasn't a dog. It was a man, or at least a human of some sort, and it came scrambling down here."

"Then where did it go?" Weaver said, raising a skeptical eyebrow.

June hesitated, before turning and looking over at the doorway that led to the steps. She made her way over and shone the flashlight down into the depths further beneath the chamber, but she wasn't quite able to give voice to her worst fears.

"Really?" Weaver said. "Are you seriously suggesting that someone went down there?"

"How much of this place did you say you'd explored?" she asked.

"There's a lot still to do," he told her, "but I can assure you that no-one has been lurking down in those tunnels. Stella and I have been here for a while, and no-one could have survived down there without us having seen them. It's simply not possible. They'd need food and water!"

"What if there's another way in and out?" June asked.

"There's isn't," Weaver told her. "Do you know how I found this site in the first place? I saw the possible outline of a structure when I was looking at some overhead images that were taken during the Second World War. I scoured those images night and day for months on end, and if there was another entrance I'd have found it by now. Besides, it would make absolutely no sense for the entrance to somehow be down there, it'd mean that this tomb violates the most basic ideas that are present in sites all around the world."

June turned to him.

"It'd mean that the entire place was almost... upside-down. And call me crazy, but I'm fairly sure that a tomb can't be upside-down."

June opened her mouth to reply, but for a moment no words came out.

"I'm going back to bed," Weaver said, turning and heading away from the chamber. "Sorry, Sister June, there'll be no hard feelings in the morning but I really need to get some shut-eye. Believe me, if I don't manage some beauty sleep, I'll be even uglier when the sun comes up." As he disappeared from view, he was still muttering away to himself, although his words were now impossible to make out.

"If it helps," Stella said after a moment, "*I* believe you."

June looked over at her.

"I'm not saying it was some tunnel-dwelling human," Stella continued, "but I also don't think you're the kind of person to get dreams and the real world mixed up." She looked down the steps again, watching the darkness at the bottom for a few seconds. "I don't like to admit it," she added, "but something about this whole site really doesn't add up. I keep coming back to the fact that Dad and I can't find the entrance. We come in and out through a hole in the ceiling, but there should be some kind of proper entrance, and there just isn't. How is that even possible?"

"I'm certainly the wrong person to ask," June pointed out.

She waited for Stella to reply, but after a few seconds she realized that something seemed to be wrong.

"If there's something worrying you," she continued cautiously, worried about overstepping the mark, "I hope you know that you can talk to me."

"Sometimes I think Dad's over-extended himself," she admitted. "Sometimes I think he'd pushing too hard and that this whole site is just some leftover from a dead-end in the history of civilization. And then sometimes..."

Her voice trailed off for a few seconds.

"Sometimes," she added finally, "I think the opposite, and I wonder whether he's genuinely stumbled upon something that might fundamentally change our understanding of human history forever. And the worst part is, I'm really not sure which of those possibilities leaves me feeling the most terrified."

CHAPTER NINE

THE FOLLOWING MORNING, WITH the sun having risen and baking heat having returned to the campsite, June held up a hand to shield her eyes as she watched a plane flying past in the distance.

"Mail carriers."

She turned to see that Stella was watching from nearby, holding a steaming cup of tea.

"The plane," Stella continued. "We see them occasionally. They're almost always carrying mail down to the south, probably to some of the areas around the Gulf of Guinea."

"I suppose I was just enjoying the sight of... civilization," June admitted.

"What's wrong? Are you worried you'll find it's all gone when you try to leave?"

"It's an irrational fear, I know."

"Not necessarily," Stella continued. "If there's one thing that archaeology has taught me, it's that civilizations *do* fall eventually. Even the biggest ones. I know it seems impossible to us now, but it would've seemed impossible once to someone in Ancient Rome or Babylon that their own civilizations would fall. Then there's nothing left but dust and ruins for the next people to find."

"Well," June said with a grimace, "when you put it like that..."

"Do you know what's funny about tea?" Stella asked, as a smile reached her lips. "It's a hot drink, but no matter where I am in the world, even in the hottest desert or jungle, somehow I feel like it's cooling me down." She took a moment to blow on the tea's surface, before taking a gentle sip that was clearly still a little too hot. "It doesn't make sense, does it?" she pointed out. "I suppose it just goes to show how the human perspective can trump reality any old day."

June smiled, but a moment later she turned to see that Weaver was already heading over to the hole in the ground.

"There's no time to waste!" he called out to them both. "I don't know about you two, but I have a date with our mummified friend down there, and I don't want to miss a second. I'm hoping that today's going to be the day I really uncover some answers about who built this place and why!"

"He's got a point," Stella said, rolling her eyes. "Are you coming?"

"Seeing as I'm still here for at least another day, I suppose I should," June admitted, although in truth she was starting to wonder just how much longer she was expected to hang around. Hadn't she already got enough to report back to the First Order? "Let's hope that you and your father are able to make some good progress today."

***

"There are some signs of violence here," Weaver muttered later, as he leaned a little further into the sarcophagus and used some tweezers to move a section of fabric aside. "Do you see his shoulder? It's been cut almost clean through."

"That must have hurt," Stella replied.

"Thank you for that valuable insight," he continued. "The cut appears to have been fairly ragged, in fact it almost looks to me as if there are two separate wounds, possibly after he was hit by some kind of bladed implement. For now, I'm going to go with the assumption that it was an ax."

"Do you think that happened before or after he died?"

"Impossible to say at this juncture," he admitted. "I wouldn't have thought that such an injury would come about in his daily life, it's more likely to have been the result of an attack. It's also more than enough for him to have bled to death, so this wound tentatively supports my conjecture that he was some kind of warrior."

"Looks that way," Stella said, before turning and glancing across the chamber.

Sister June was still standing at the arched doorway that led down to the steps and further into the darker, mostly unexplored sections of the site. She'd been there for a few minutes now, and Stella couldn't help but wonder what she found so fascinating.

"Are you alright there, Sister?" she called out.

"Hmm?"

June turned to her, clearly a little surprised to hear her own name.

"Oh, I'm quite alright," she stammered. "I'm just thinking, really, and trying to keep out of your way."

"You're more than welcome to come and take a look with us," Stella told her.

"I try to be as discreet as possible," June explained. "Your work is the most important thing here, and I certainly would hate to get in the way. Honestly, I'm quite happy just looking around and getting a sense of the place. Please don't mind me. If you'd prefer, I could go back up to the surface."

"No, you're fine there," Stella told her. "Just

come over in a while if you feel like it."

"You're most kind," June said, before holding up her notebook. "I'll just stick to observing, if that's alright with you. I tend to find that observing is more my natural area of expertise."

Stepping around to the other side of the sarcophagus, Stella tilted her head as she looked at the side of the mummified figure's head. She'd never entirely become accustomed to the idea of poking around with dead bodies, even if they'd been gone for hundreds or even thousands of years; she couldn't quite escape the fact that this had been a person once, with a life and probably a family and a job and hopes and dreams. As she watched her father lifting another section of fabric so that he could examine the man's chest, she felt a shiver pass through her bones, but she knew that there was no point raising any of her concerns.

After all, the great Doctor Mortimer Weaver wasn't exactly known for his sense of tact or caution.

"I wish I could decipher these markings on the inside of the sarcophagus," he said after a moment. "They're on the walls, too. They're everywhere. It's so frustrating knowing that there's potentially so much information here, yet we're powerless to know what it says."

"Some of the text looks familiar

sometimes," Stella admitted, "but only for a few moments at a time. I'm not sure that the language used here is *entirely* different to the more common languages we're used to."

"Feel free to spend some more time trying to decipher it."

"I'm not too good at that sort of thing," she reminded him. "I prefer to get my hands dirty. Sister June took a rubbing of some of the lines, I suppose it's possible that her religious mind might have more luck."

She glanced over her shoulder and saw June still staring down the steps, and then she turned to her father again.

"Actually," she continued, lowering her voice to a conspiratorial whisper, "I still don't really understand what she's doing here. Do you have any idea who the First Order are?"

"Not the foggiest."

"And you're not concerned?"

"I'm *very* concerned," he told her, "but what would you have me do? Tie the woman down and interrogate her? I sense that she knows precious little more than we do." He glanced over at June, before looking back down at the mummified corpse. "I intend to get on with my work, and deal with any possible interruptions later. I must admit, I have a bad feeling about this First Order business, but there's absolutely nothing I can do about it right now. I'm going to review my communications with England, however. Evidently those aren't quite as secure as I'd hoped."

"Just the name First Order gives me the creeps," Stella said. "It sounds like something pretty menacing, if you ask me." She thought for a moment, but the sense of concern still wouldn't quite leave her thoughts. "In a film they'd be the bad guys, for sure," she added. "You know what I'm like, Dad, I hate any kind of organized authority, and this First Order bunch really sound like they might be into telling people what to do."

"People the world over seem to have that impulse."

"Sure, but it's when they get really organized that I don't like it. I mean, what kind of organization flies nuns around the world and gets them to observe people on archaeological digs? Don't you think that something about this entire set-up feels really... wrong? How do we even know that she's really a nun, anyway?"

She looked over her shoulder, and then she froze as she saw the empty doorway. She glanced around, but she already knew that there was no way Sister June could possibly have gone back to the surface without walking straight past, which meant that there was only one possible explanation. Hurrying to the doorway, she looked down the steps and still saw no sign of anyone, and then she turned to her father again.

"Dad, she's gone!" she exclaimed. "The nun! I've got no idea why, but I think she might have gone down to the lower level!"

CHAPTER TEN

"WELCOME, SISTER JUNE," THE voice continued, speaking to June from the darkness ahead as she made her way along the tunnel with just her flashlight to pick out the route. "We've been expecting you for a long time."

"But who are you?" she asked, lost in a daze as she stepped over some rocks on the ground. "Why won't you answer my questions?"

"This is where you belong."

"I -"

"This is where you've always belonged. You know that, deep down, if you search your soul. You know it's true."

"I have no idea what you -"

"Since Holdham Hall," the voice added. "Since you were young. You've always known that you belong down here with us."

Stopping suddenly, June opened her mouth to reply, but those two words – Holdham Hall – had already sent a shiver of fear through her chest. She blinked, and in her mind's eye she could see that place again after so many years, complete with its huge windows running up to the high ceiling, and the old school photographs no doubt still on the walls. She'd tried not to think of the place for so very long, but she knew deep down that it was out there somewhere, waiting for her in the English countryside.

"How... how do you know about that place?" she whispered, her voice trembling with fear.

"We know all about you. We always have. We noticed you when you were still very young."

"You have no right to be talking to me about this," she replied defiantly, as she felt tears starting to fill her eyes. "Do you understand? My past is my past, and it has nothing to do with the present."

"Oh, but that's where you're wrong," the voice continued, and now it sounded almost as if it was starting to laugh. "Haven't you ever wondered why *you* were chosen for this path? Haven't you ever stopped to question what it is about you that makes you so perfect to come and join us down here in -"

"Sister June?"

Startled, June let out a shocked gasp as she spun around. She dropped her flashlight and notebook, sending pages spilling out as she stepped back against the wall. Only now did she realize that she recognized Stella Weaver staring back at her with a shocked, somewhat baffled expression on her face.

"I'm sorry," Stella said, "I tried to get through to you several times but it was like you didn't hear me."

"I was..."

June hesitated, before looking further along the tunnel. She saw only darkness, and she heard only the sound of her own panicked breaths.

"Did you hear it?" she asked.

"Hear what?"

"The voice?"

"What voice?"

June turned to Stella again, and in that moment she realized that the voice hadn't been real at all, that it had only existed in her head. That thought made her feel a little better, at least, although she was shocked that after so many years her mind had chosen this of all moments to bring up Holdham Hall again. A few seconds later, looking down, she saw her flashlight on the floor with the notebook pages a little further away.

"I'm sorry," she said, crouching down to pick the flashlight up, then grabbing the notebook.

"I don't quite know what came over me."

"When I realized you were gone, I got worried," Stella explained. "You're in a part of the site that Dad hasn't explored yet. We don't even know that it's safe."

"Evidently," June said, feeling increasingly flustered as she stood up and tried to straighten her notes. "I'm so sorry, I really didn't mean to bother you. I think I just... I came down here to take a look around, that's all. Yes, that's it, I came to have a look and see what I might find. It's really not a big thing, and I can assure you that it won't happen again." She stepped past Stella. "We should go back up."

"You missed one," Stella said, picking up a stray page from the notebook and then looking at it for a moment. Seeing the rubbing June had made of the strange lettering, she furrowed her brow for a few seconds as at last something began to make sense. "Hey," she continued, "do you want to know something? I think you might just have helped us figure this whole thing out."

***

"This is utterly, utterly absurd and ridiculous," Weaver said, standing in the chamber as he stared at the page from June's notebook. He paused, before turning the page the other way up. "And yet, at the same time, so wonderfully simple and brilliant."

"I only noticed because the page was upside-down when I picked it up," Stella told him.

"Would one of you mind telling me what's going on?" June asked, trying to keep from sounding irritated. "I'm afraid I'm really not following any of this whatsoever."

"It's gonna sound really loopy," Stella replied, before pausing for a moment as she tried to work out how to explain the situation. "There are lots of ways that we try to identify a new language, usually by finding connections and patterns linking them to things we already understand. The truth is, new languages don't really pop up that often. The text in this tomb, however, has seemed completely alien until today. When I picked up the rubbing you made, I was holding it upside-down, and suddenly it all fitted."

"Upside-down?" June said, as if she couldn't quite believe that it could all be so simple. "Is that all it took?"

"We're not there yet," Stella explained, "but Dad and I are both starting to notice certain elements that might be familiar."

"So why would the text all over the tomb be upside-down?" June asked.

"That's the million dollar question," Stella countered, before letting out a sigh. "It's all so obvious, but at the same time it wasn't obvious at all until... well, until it was. It's one of those things that's got us kicking ourselves now."

"This part makes some sense," Weaver said, running a finger-tip along the page from June's notebook. "I've seen something like this before. It's..."

His voice trailed off, and then he looked up at his daughter.

"It's a warning."

"About the tomb?" Stella asked.

"I think this is one of your common or garden warnings about not disturbing the tomb," he continued. "In itself, it's not that interesting, but it could pave the way for us to understand the other inscriptions in here. That's what makes it so exciting."

"What kind of warning?" June said cautiously.

"Relax," Stella replied, "you always get them on tombs. It'll just be threatening all sorts of consequences for anyone who breaks in and disturbs the body. Blah blah, right? It's really nothing to worry about or even pay attention to."

"How can you be sure of that?" June asked.

"Because we're standing here right now and we're perfectly fine?" Stella suggested. "That's the big giveaway. These warnings were intended for people in more superstitious times who would actually have worried about things like curses and the undead. To those of us in the more enlightened modern age, they're really nothing more than an amusing curiosity." She reached over and patted June on the back. "Thank you, Sister June. I know it was a bit of an accident, but you've potentially saved us months and months of work."

June almost replied, but for a few seconds she thought back to the voice she'd heard down in the tunnel. Something about that voice had left her feeling terribly unsettled, and after a moment she turned and looked back at the doorway that led to the steps. She thought of the inscription carved on the wall, and of the way she'd had to stand when she'd made the rubbing, and for a few more seconds nothing quite seem to add up. Something was gnawing at her thoughts, and finally she understood exactly what was wrong.

"Isn't it in the wrong place?" she whispered.

"What was that?" Stella asked airily, having already returned her attention to the notebook page.

"The warning," June continued, before turning to her. "I'm no expert on these things, but isn't the warning in a rather unusual place?"

"What do you mean?" Stella replied cautiously.

"I would have thought that something like that would be on the outside of the tomb, to try to stop people venturing inside," June continued. "In that case... what's it doing at the *top* of that set of steps?"

Stella opened her mouth to reply, but at the last second she held back. Finally, slowly, she too turned and looked at the doorway, as if she too understood that something about the warning still made absolutely no sense whatsoever.

CHAPTER ELEVEN

"OKAY, SO... YOU'VE GOT a point," Stella said as she and June stood on the steps and looked at the carved text all around the arched doorway. "Maybe."

"It just seems to me," June continued, "that the only way this warning would work, would be if the person seeking to enter the tomb was coming from..."

Her voice trailed off, and after a few seconds she turned and looked over her shoulder. For a moment she stared into the darkness below.

"From down there," she added finally.

She waited for Stella to correct her, for the archaeology expert to step in with a perfectly reasonable explanation. When this didn't happen, she turned to see a puzzled expression on Stella's face.

"Is there perhaps another way in?" June asked, hoping to perhaps stumble upon a solution.

"Dad studied those aerial photos pretty carefully," Stella told her. "It's just not feasible for that there to be another entrance, especially not one that goes down so far before coming up again. Think about it, what would be the point?"

"Then we come back to this warning," June continued, "which seems to be directed squarely at somebody coming *up* these steps. The question is, where would those people be coming from? Because if they're not coming from the surface..."

"We need to go down there and take a proper look," Stella said after a moment, with a trace of dread in her voice. "But June, we need to be careful what we tell my father. Because if he thinks for one second that we're going off on some flight of fancy, he'll shoot us down so fast our heads'll be spinning."

***

"Just wait one moment," June said a short while later, stopping in one of the tunnels and adding some more lines to the drawing in her notebook. "I need to make sure that I get this right."

"Yeah, that'd be nice," Stella replied. "I'd definitely rather not get lost down here, thanks very much."

"So far, so good," June muttered, double-checking that the map was correct, "although I still don't understand why we have to be so secretive. Couldn't we just have told your father why we came down here?"

"Dad's a contradictory character at the best of times," Stella said, aiming her flashlight ahead as they resumed their walk along the tunnel. "Sometimes he wants to go pushing on ahead, and other times he's far more cautious."

"When you're involved?"

Stella glanced at her.

"I've seen the pattern before," June admitted with a faint smile. "A father is more than willing to blunder into things and put his own life at risk, but when it comes to a son or a daughter, he absolutely won't condone the same type of behavior."

"Dad's never exactly been the protective parent type."

"One never knows how that impulse will manifest itself," June countered. "Anyway, he seemed happy enough with the idea that you were coming to help me find something I dropped down here, although I find myself wondering how long he'll give us."

"He's all wrapped up in that mummy," Stella pointed out. "Sorry, bad choice of words, but you get the idea. He won't even notice how much time is passing up there, he's far too engrossed in his work." Stopping at a junction, she shone the flashlight first to the left and then to the right. "Story of my childhood," she continued. "The big question is which way should we go next?"

"And what about your mother?" June asked as she added to her map.

"She died years ago, on a dig," Stella explained. "Relax, it was nothing terribly exciting. They were way down south and she got malaria. Dad couldn't save her and she died there. I was just a little kid at the time, I'd been left behind in England at a boarding school. To be honest, I kind of just got on with things. I was too busy studying and fighting off classroom bullies to spend much time on childhood trauma." She glanced at June. "Dad blames himself, though. He'd never admit it, but I can tell."

"I'm sorry you had to go though that," June replied. "It must have been hard."

"So this is turning out to be way more labyrinthine than I ever imagined," Stella said, clearly keen to change the subject as she once again shone the flashlight's beam around. "It's one thing to have a tunnel down here, but this is more like a small town. Well, not a town exactly, but you get the idea. It's a proper little complex, all buried far beneath the surface and so far everything seems to be sloping downward."

"Almost like an entire underground world," June said.

She waited for Stella to continue, before turning to see that she seemed lost in thought.

"Not that I'm suggesting such a thing," she added. "Obviously that would be absurd."

"Not if you believe the stories," Stella whispered, before turning to her. "In some of the ancient texts left behind by the earliest civilizations, there's mention of a group of people who lived exclusively beneath the surface, never coming up to see the sun. It's a crazy idea that's been pretty much ignored by every mainstream archaeologist in the game, but one thing that always puzzled me was the consistency of the claims."

"Do you mean a few unusual people lived a kind of subterranean existence?" June asked.

"No, I mean way more than that," Stella told her. "If you believe the stories – and I'm not saying that I do – but if you wanted to delve into them, you'd find references to an entire civilization that supposedly existed completely underground. They were only ever encountered by surface-dwellers who ventured too deep into cave systems, and those encounters tended not to be too peaceful. From what I remember of the literature, the underground people weren't too keen on meeting anyone from the surface."

"Okay," June said cautiously, "but you said

that the idea had been dismissed by all the experts. A few unexplained tunnels in the middle of the Sahara doesn't mean that there's actually something down here that was missed by everyone else."

"I know," Stella said, as they set off again along another tunnel, with June already adding more detail to her map, "and Dad would absolutely rip me a new one if he heard me mentioning this stuff. To be honest, I was always kind of entertained by the idea of an entire massive subterranean civilization that rose and fell beneath the ground, although I never truly believed it might be possible. If the stories are to be believed, these people built entire cities miles and miles beneath the surface."

"Surely those would have been found by now, would they not?" June suggested.

She waited for an answer, but Stella was picking up the pace now and June struggled to keep up.

"Something like that couldn't stay hidden for long in the modern age," June continued. "The idea's just not credible."

"It's unlikely," Stella agreed, "but that doesn't mean it's impossible. Believe me, I know from experience that human beings are really lousy at working out what's possible and what's not. Hell, once up a time even something as basic as a telephone or a plane would have been dismissed by some people as impossible."

"Should we perhaps slow down?" June suggested, scribbling in her notebook again. "I'd really like to make extra sure that I'm getting everything noted down correctly."

"This part seems to be just a straight line," Stella pointed out. "That shouldn't be too hard to draw."

"Well, I know, but -"

"Sister, are you scared?" Stella asked, stopping suddenly and turning to aim the flashlight at her.

Almost bumping into her, June stopped and had to protect her eyes from the flashlight's beam.

"Because it's okay if you are," Stella continued. "You can go back up, if you prefer. I get that charging around down here isn't everyone's cup of tea."

"I'm quite alright with that," June replied, still keen to avoid dwelling on the voice she'd heard earlier. She looked around for a moment, but she had to admit that now the tunnels were completely still and quiet. "I'm fine, in fact," she added. "I just want to make sure that we do things methodically, that's all."

"Despite my father's assertions," Stella said as they started walking again, "I actually know what I'm doing. He seems to think that I rely on him completely, whereas I'm more than capable of leading my own digs by now. He thinks he's helping my career by bringing me along, but I see it the other way round. He's old and he's sick, and I'm helping him by accompanying him." She stopped and turned to look at June again, aiming her flashlight past her. "At least, that's how I see it," she added. "I might be wrong, but I really feel that without me, he might miss something like this."

"Indeed," June said, before furrowing her brow. "I beg your pardon, but... something like *what*?"

"Like that," Stella replied, nodding past her.

Confused, June turned and looked at the opposite wall. In that moment, she felt a shudder pass through her body as she found herself staring at a large and very elaborately-decorated stone gate.

CHAPTER TWELVE

"THIS IS BEAUTIFUL," STELLA said, reaching out and touching the detailed carvings on the gate's side. "Look at it. Such rich imagery and such amazing patterns."

"What's it doing down here?" June asked, hanging back a little. "I mean... who could have built such a thing?"

"Anyone with a little time and expertise," Stella replied, before stepping through the gate and turning to look at its other side. "There's a lot of text on here. Some of the stuff on this side looks very familiar, I think it might be a warning like the stuff you found before."

"And it's on the wrong side again," June pointed out. "Wrong from our perspective, at least."

"Exactly," Stella said, touching another set

of carvings. "It's warning someone from below not to come up too close to the surface."

"Could it perhaps be a joke?" June suggested.

Stella glanced at her.

"A practical joke from long ago," June continued, although she knew that her idea already sounded rather flimsy. "Someone wanted to leave a little puzzle for future generations who might come wandering along. I know that seems unlikely, but one never quite knows what people might get up to when they've been left to their own devices."

"I suppose nothing can be entirely ruled out," Stella admitted, "but there's another idea I've been toying with for a while, although it seems almost too bizarre to be true."

"I rather specialize in the bizarre," June said with a sigh. "Not by choice, of course."

She looked up at the top of the gate, which rose several feet above her head, and she felt a shiver as she wondered who could possibly have built such a thing so deep beneath the desert. Until that moment she'd more or less dismissed Stella's talk of subterranean civilizations, but now she found herself wondering whether this might be why the First Order had sent her in the first place; a secret civilization, unknown to mankind for thousands of years, certainly seemed to be something the First Order would find interesting, even if she herself felt utterly ill-equipped to make any judgment whatsoever on such a monumental topic.

"This is a threshold," Stella said finally. "I'm really struggling to make much headway with the text, but if it works the way I'm starting to think that it does, then there's a warning up here." She pointed toward one section of the gate. "I think it might say that this is the fifth gate or... fifth tomb, something like that."

"And what might that mean?" June asked, starting to feel a little chilly in the deep subterranean passage.

"Your guess is as good as mine," Stella replied, turning and aiming her flashlight ahead, picking out a wide sloping corridor that clearly ran further underground. "This whole complex might extend for miles," she pointed out. "There's no way the two of us can explore it on our own. You'd need a whole army to map the place out. I think perhaps it's time to admit that we've bitten off more than we can chew. Even Dad's going to have to admit that -"

Stopping suddenly, she took a step forward.

"What's wrong?" June asked.

"Did you see that?" Stella replied.

"I didn't see -"

"Hello?" Stella shouted, her voice echoing loudly. "Is someone there?"

"I didn't see anyone," June said firmly.

"Something moved up there," Stella

continued, taking a few more steps forward. "I know you probably think I'm crazy, but I swear to God I saw a figure moving in the shadows. Sorry, I hope I didn't just take anyone's name in vain there."

"It's so hard to see," June replied, making her way over to join Stella, then shining her own flashlight ahead.

"You thought you saw someone in the night," Stella reminded her. "I'll be honest, I really wasn't convinced, but now I'm starting to wonder whether you might have been onto something." She took another step forward. "If there's anyone here," she continued, "I really just want to talk to you. We're friendly, we're only exploring and we just want to understand what we've found. There's really no reason for you to be afraid."

They both waited, but they heard no answer until – a few seconds later – footsteps rang out far away deeper in the corridor.

"You heard that, right?" Stella said cautiously.

"I'm afraid I did," June replied

"Wait!" Stella yelled, hurrying forward as the footsteps faded into the distance. "We really just want to help. Please, can't you at least talk to us?"

June waited, but after a moment she realized that Stella was getting too far ahead. Rushing to catch up, she quickly made some more notes on her map, although she was really having to get things done quickly now and she worried that she might be on the verge of making mistakes.

"I think we should slow down a little," she told Stella. "Please, if -"

"Wait for us!" Stella shouted, breaking into a jog and pulling away from June, aiming her flashlight straight ahead while waving frantically. "Please don't run away, we're friendly and we only want to talk to you!"

June almost dropped her notebook, and she felt a rush of relief as she saw that Stella had stopped up ahead. Once she caught up to the younger woman, she saw that the passage continued in the same manner as far as the eye could see, with no hint of any kind of turning or other way out.

"We could get completely lost down here," Stella said finally, sounding a little out of breath now. "How's the map going?"

"It's accurate so far, I think," June replied, looking at her scribbles. "No, I'm sure it's right. I can definitely get us back to the surface."

"I might be hot-headed," Stella replied, "but I'm not a complete idiot. There's no way I'm going to just go charging into this place. Do you mind if I borrow your notebook for a moment?"

Reaching over, she took the book and wrote a few lines, before tearing the page out and setting it on the floor.

"There's not exactly a breeze to blow it

away," she pointed out. "I doubt anyone down here understands English, but it's worth a shot. I've just written a few words emphasizing the fact that we want to make peaceful contact, and hopefully they'll be able to get the gist." She stared along the tunnel for a moment longer before slowly getting to her feet and turning to June. "I suppose it's possible that some tribe from the surface found its way down here and decided to use the pre-existing tunnels. My hunch, though, is that something else is going on here. The person I saw just now, or who I *think* I saw..."

She paused, as if she was too afraid to complete that sentence.

"I don't know," she continued, "I might be wrong, but it didn't look quite... the way I'd expect a human to look, if you catch my drift."

"I think I do," June said cautiously, "although I'm not sure that I like the implications very much."

"We're going to have to head back up," Stella explained, as they turned and began to make their way toward the gate. "We're so completely not equipped to go exploring, and besides, even Dad's going to notice that we're missing eventually. Actually, June, there's one other thing I need you to do for me. A favor, if you like." Stopping at the gate, she turned to June. "Dad's never going to buy into some of the stuff we've seen down here. Just for the rest of today, would you mind not mentioning the crazier ideas I've been coming up with you? I'd rather avoid having to waste time defending the fact that we saw something moving, or the idea that we might have stumbled upon evidence of an ancient subterranean civilization. I'm not asking you to lie, exactly, just... can you omit certain details?"

"Lying certainly isn't something that I would ever do lightly," June told her, "but I suppose it's hardly my place to offer a commentary on these matters. You're the archaeologist, Stella, so I rather think you should be the one to tell your father's what has been going on."

"Thanks," Stella replied awkwardly. "I'll tell Dad the truth, I swear, but I need a little more thinking time first. I have to figure out the best way to proceed, and Dad's judgment is too clouded at the moment by his health problems. What matters is what's best for the site as a whole. Even Dad will realize that eventually."

"It's clear that you've found something very significant here," June admitted.

"Significant might be an understatement," Stella continued. "If I'm right about everything, this discovery might completely change the way we view the history of humanity."

CHAPTER THIRTEEN

"THIS IS THE MOST ridiculous thing I've ever heard in my life!" Weaver spluttered as he sat on a fold-out chair in the tent above-ground. "A gate? All the way down there?"

"I know it might be difficult to believe," Stella said, as she showed him another of the sketches she'd made showing the subterranean gate, "but it's true."

"What are you going to try to get me to believe next?" he muttered, taking the sketch and peering at it for a moment. "Little men running around down there?"

Stella glanced at June, then back to her father.

"It shouldn't be *that* hard to get your head around," she said cautiously. "We found the tomb, and the steps, and now it turns out that this complex extends much further underground than we ever thought." She passed him the page showing June's tentative map. "This is the section we explored. There wasn't much down there, I get the feeling that we were on just a passageway running from one location to another. If I'm right, there could be so much more to discover down there."

"This is all just a little hard to wrap my head around," Weaver replied, setting the papers aside and then removing his glasses before taking a moment to rub the corners of his eyes. "Of course I always dreamed about making a discovery like this, every archaeologist does, but to have it actually happen, especially toward the end of -"

He caught himself just in time.

"I'm just not sure that I can comprehend the magnitude of it all," he added, with a hint of defeat in his weary voice. Looking at his daughter again as he put his glasses back in place, he seemed lost for words. "Stella, my dear, do you even understand how important this might be? All our knowledge of human history, of the cradle of life and the birth of the earliest civilizations, is at risk. If this place is real, and if it's as old as I suspect it might be, we could be talking about a lost world. And the fact that it all seems to have been underground..."

Clearly unable to finish that sentence, he stared at Stella as if he was hoping that she'd come up with a solution.

"I'm going to carry out some more checks," she told him, "and then -"

"No," he replied, cutting her off.

"Dad, if -"

"This isn't the time for two idiots to go running around underground," he insisted, before turning to June. "I'm sorry, Sister, where are my manners? I didn't mean to leave you out." He looked at Stella again. "This isn't the time for three idiots to go running around underground," he said, correcting himself. "We've hit the end of the road for our own personal dig, and it's time for us to turn this site over to the big boys. I imagine all the leading archaeologists from around the world will be desperate to take charge of the site. I'm sorry if that's not how you imagined things working, but I'm sure I can wangle you a job with them."

"As someone's assistant?" Stella suggested wryly, before sighing. "It's okay, Dad, I know you're right. I just want to spend a little longer looking around this place without interference before we turn it over. Is that too much to ask?" She waited for an answer, and her father was already clearly torn over his decision. "Please, Dad?" she continued. "One more day?"

"Sometimes you remind me so much of myself," he said, with tears in his eyes, "and sometimes you remind me so much of your mother."

"Does that mean you agree?"

He hesitated, and then he nodded.

"One more day," he told her, although he sounded as if he regretted the words even as they left his mouth. "We'll re-assess things tomorrow and then perhaps we'll have to signal for a pick-up a little ahead of time. Our next supplies are due at the end of the week, but I'm not sure we should wait that long. We've got the flare-gun, we can always use it to attract the attention of one of those mail planes if necessary."

"Thank you," Stella replied, leaning over and kissing him on the cheek. "You won't regret this, Dad. I promise."

***

"I've made a terrible mistake," Weaver said later, as he sat stirring some soup while the sun began to set on the horizon. "I should never have indulged that girl."

"She seems to have her head screwed on pretty well," June suggested.

Hearing the sound of equipment clattering out of a box, she turned to see that Stella had dropped some tools. She watched for a moment as the younger woman crouched down to pick things up, and then she turned to Weaver again.

"She's young and enthusiastic," she pointed out. "I don't know about you, but I certainly remember what it was like to feel that way."

"And I'm supposed to be the guiding hand and the voice of reason," he replied, clearly still worried. "I promised her mother that I'd look after her, and I'm fairly sure that doesn't mean letting her loose in some underground tunnels."

"You can't protect her forever."

"I'm painfully aware of that fact, thank you," he replied quickly, clearly irked by the suggestion. "I'm sorry," he added, "I didn't mean that to sound so harsh. It's just that I always wanted her to get her big break in archaeology, but I never anticipated that it might be *this* big."

"For what it's worth," June said, "I think she'll cope just fine. With the work side of things, I mean."

"To be honest with you," he continued, "we couldn't have called for a pick-up this late in the day anyway, so staying until tomorrow was less of a choice on my part and more of an admission of the situation. We've packed up now and I suppose Stella will want to explore some more in the morning, but after that I think I'm going to have to have our transport come to collected us all. That includes you too, Sister, by the way."

"I would be most obliged," she told him.

"Then this whole site will be turned over to

all sorts of competing idiots," he added with a sigh, "and progress will slow to a crawl. We'll all be lucky if we find out the truth in our lifetimes, but there's really no alternative. The resources required to explore this site are beyond anything I can access."

Hearing another clattering sound, June turned to see that Stella was struggling with some more tools.

"I think I might just go and give her a hand," she said, getting to her feet. "That is, if there's nothing I can do to help you here..."

"Go and help her," Weaver replied, rolling his eyes. "I think she might need it."

As she made her way over, June felt a cool breeze blowing against her face. The heat of the desert was fading already, and she knew that she was in for another cold night.

"Did Dad send you to help me?" Stella asked, picking up some more tools from the sand.

"No," June said with a faint smile, "I simply saw you struggling so I thought I'd offer to assist you in any way that might be necessary."

"I'm completely fine, thank you," Stella insisted. "Dad always thinks that I can't handle things, but I've never once dropped the ball." As those words left her lips, a knife fell from the bundle of tools in her arms; June reached down and picked it up, before setting it on the nearby table.

"That wasn't a ball," Stella reminded her. "It was a knife. Big difference."

"Your father only has your best interests at heart," June told her. "I know it's only natural for a child to want to prove to their parent that they're capable, but I hope you don't think your father doubts you. I think it's more the case that he's very realistic about the challenges you're both facing here."

"You didn't tell him about the thing we saw moving, did you?"

"I did not," June replied, "and I hope you won't give me cause to regret that omission."

"Whatever's down there is clearly terrified of us," Stella explained. "We've been here for longer than you have, Sister June. *Much* longer. If anything wanted to hurt us, it could easily have done so by now." She set the bundle of tools down, and then she dusted her hands for a moment before turning to June again. "So don't worry about a thing, Sister June," she added with a faint, confident smile. "We've got everything here completely and totally under control."

AMY CROSS

CHAPTER FOURTEEN

HER NAME WAS ELOISE Tate, and as she stood in the hallway of her parents' house just outside Zurich, she looked down at the plain white envelope she'd just propped on the table next to the phone.

A solitary tear ran from her left eyes as she imagined them opening that envelope when they got back from their vacation. She thought of them reading what she'd written, then reading it again, then again and again as they tried to make sense of everything; she thought of their disbelief and panic, of all the phone-calls they were going to make, first to her phone and then to her friends, and then finally to the police. She thought of the nightmarish hours that would pass between them reading that letter and them discovering that every word it contained was true.

And as she thought of those things, she knew that she had no choice. This was just how things were going to have to be.

"I'm sorry," she whispered, keeping her voice low even though she knew there was nobody else in the house. "I know you tried. You tried so hard, it's just... I don't think it was ever going to be possible to help me. You didn't do anything wrong, it's just that you could never succeed."

She briefly considered opening the envelope and rewriting the letter, but at the last moment she realized that there was no point, and that she had to act fast before her bravery evaporated; she hurried to the front door and pulled it open, and then she stepped outside and pulled the door shut. Having intentionally left the keys inside, she now had no way of going back on her decision; her parents *would* discover the letter when they returned from their vacation, so now she simply had to go through with the one act that had been on her mind for so long now.

"I'm sorry," she said softly, with tears in her eyes as she hurried up the steps and away along the sloping road that led back into the city.

***

Loud, drunk voices were calling out from the arched doorways that led into various bars and clubs. As Eloise made her way down the steep cobbled street, she felt the pull of those late-night hostelries, but she knew she needed to stay sober. She understood only too well, from bitter personal experience, how a few drinks could snowball into a few dozen and then she'd end up passing out.

The last thing she needed, she told herself, was to see another sunrise.

"Alright there?" a woman asked drunkenly, leaning against the door of one of the seedier bars. "Want to come inside and try your luck?"

"No, thank you," Eloise murmured.

"Are you sure?" the woman continued. "A pretty thing like you shouldn't have any trouble getting people to buy her drinks all night."

"Thank you, but I'm fine," Eloise said firmly, even though part of her desperately wanted to take up that offer. "I have to be somewhere."

Picking up the pace, she hurried around the next corner, only to slam straight into a man coming the other way. Startled, she stepped back and opened her mouth to apologize, but in that instant she heard a faint grunt coming from the man's lips, and she was suddenly overcome by the strangest scent she'd ever encountered in her life. It wasn't that the man had a bad smell, not at all; rather, something about his fragrance didn't seem quite human, as if deep down Eloise's senses were picking up on something that her conscious mind

AMY CROSS

couldn't see.

"Sorry," she stammered finally, feeling deeply embarrassed as she stepped past the man. "I wasn't looking where I was doing."

She managed one more step before she felt his hand grip her arm. She froze, wanting to pull away, but something about this man's touch sent a tingle through her body; he felt huge, almost like a bear, and when she turned to him she saw a hint of darkness in his eyes. Once again, she was left at a loss for words.

"I'm sorry," he said, releasing his grip on her arm. "I shouldn't have done that. It's just that for a moment, you reminded me of someone else."

Eloise smiled, although she really wasn't in the mood to talk to anyone.

"Isn't it a little late for you to be out alone?" he asked, before sighing. "Wait, I forgot, these days women are a lot more adventurous. You probably think that I sound desperately old-fashioned."

"I -"

"My name's John," he continued, offering his hand for her to shake. "I'm just in town for a short visit. I have a few... jobs that I need to get done."

"I hope you enjoy your time here," she replied, and she was frustrated now by the fear she could hear in her own voice.

"I'm not sure enjoyment is really my

priority," he explained, before hesitating and then – with no warning – leaning a little closer.

"Whatever you're here for," Eloise replied nervously, "I hope it works out for you. Zurich is really a lovely city for anyone who..."

Again her voice trailed off, and she was starting to notice a persistent low sniffing sound coming from the man's nose as he leaned even closer.

"Are you..."

She hesitated.

"Are you smelling me?" she asked finally.

"My apologies," he replied, pulling back. "That was terribly rude of me. You don't smell bad, not at all. It's just that I thought for a moment that I picked up on..." He paused, and then he smiled. "It's a little peculiarity of mine," he continued. "It's probably all in my head, really, but sometimes I convince myself that I have a particularly good sense of smell, and that I can even detect emotions that way. Nothing too complex, of course, just the base emotions like fear and happiness and..."

He leaned just a little closer, as if he wanted to get another sniff.

"Bravery," he added.

"I'm not brave," she told him.

"Then perhaps that was the wrong word," he admitted. "Would you mind if I try again?"

"I..."

She thought about his question for a moment, but she really didn't want to seem rude. Besides, she knew where she was going, and part of her wanted to delay that moment for a little longer.

"Sure," she said finally. "I mean... I guess."

"Thank you," he replied, before leaning closer and sniffing the side of her neck. "Okay, I get it now. I was close, but what you're actually feeling is a kind of relief. There's something you've been putting off for a while, something that's important to you, something that you think will make everything better. You've been suffering and you want that suffering to end, and you've been trying endless ways to make that happen but now finally you're sure you've made a major breakthrough. There's some fear, though, even if so far you've been managing to keep it under wraps."

"I don't know what you're talking about," she murmured, but she already knew that she sounded like a liar.

"It's happening tonight, isn't it?" he continued. "Whatever you're planning to do, I mean. You think that by the time the sun comes up in the morning, it'll all be over. You've put everything in order and you think that whatever you're going to do, it's for the best."

He pulled back and looked into her eyes.

"Wait, I'm worried about this," he added. "Are you -"

"I have to go!" she blurted out, turning and hurrying along the next alley, almost but not quite breaking into a jog. "I'm sorry," she added, even though she knew he'd no longer be able to hear her. "Really, I am, it's just that I'm late for something."

"Wait!" he called after her. "Are you going to be okay?"

Reaching the next corner, she stopped and looked back. She saw to her relief that the strange man hadn't followed her; he was standing at the spot where they'd been talking, and a nearby streetlight was casting his shadow across one of the walls. For a moment Eloise watched that shadow growing, as if it was becoming less human and more like some other kind of creature, but a few seconds later the man stepped out of view and his shadow was gone.

"I'm sorry," Eloise whispered, before setting off again, relieved that the man was leaving her alone. Something about him had shaken her to her core, and now she was more determined than ever to get back to her flat and finish things. "I don't want to be any trouble," she added, talking to herself as much as to any imagined passersby. "I just want to get out of everyone's way."

AMY CROSS

CHAPTER FIFTEEN

A FEW HOURS LATER, Stella Weaver stood shivering in the cold night air as she listened to the sound of snores coming from the tent. She was used to her father snoring, of course, but she'd been surprised to find that Sister June wasn't exactly a silent sleeper either. Fortunately, on this particular night the twin snores of her companions were proving to be very useful.

Once she was sure that the others were asleep, Stella turned and picked her way past the various tables until she reached the hole that led down into the chamber below. She felt a tightening sense of fear in her chest, and the plans she'd made during the day now seemed so much more daunting at night; at the same time, she knew that this was the only way she was ever going to get out from her father's shadow.

She glanced back toward the tent one more time, and then she began to climb down into the depths beneath the surface. At the bottom she switched her flashlight on and made her way from the foot of the ladder, until she reached the burial chamber and found herself looking down once again at the mummified body in the sarcophagus. She knew she was being foolish, but she couldn't shake the sense that the figure seemed a little more unnerving at night, even though the chamber itself remained dark during the day.

"Hey, Monty," she muttered under her breath. "Sorry, I hope you don't mind that I've nicknamed you Monty."

She watched the figure's face, and she couldn't help but wonder what he'd been like when he was alive.

"I bet you could tell some stories," she continued with a faint smile. "I mean, you're going to tell some anyway once we get you back to the lab and run some tests, but I bet if you could actually talk you'd be able to tell us so much. I wish we could communicate somehow, but..."

Her voice trailed off for a few seconds, and then she turned and aimed her flashlight's beam at the doorway that led through to the steps.

"There's something about working alone," she explained, "without having to tell someone what you're doing all the time, that feels so much more rewarding. And more efficient, too." She paused before looking down at the mummified body again. "Don't worry," she added, "I won't be long. I'll be back up before you know it, Monty."

***

Down in the tunnel system, having followed the route that June had carefully mapped out in the notebook, Stella stepped through the stone gate and found herself once again looking along the wide passageway that sloped down deeper into the darkness. She waited for a moment, just in case she might spot some sign of movement again, and then she began to make her way forward.

Her footsteps echoed all around in the cold space.

"Hello?" she called out cautiously. "I'm sorry about earlier, I hope we didn't scare you. I get it, we probably seem a little weird to you, but that doesn't have to be a bad thing. Does it?"

Soon she reached the spot where she'd left the note. Crouching down, she picked it up and realized that as far as she could tell, it had gone completely untouched. She looked ahead, and now she was starting to wonder whether the supposed movement might actually have been some strange trick of the light. Every rational and logical part of her mind told her that nothing could survive down in the tunnels, that the idea of a living creature moving about in the shadows was simply too absurd, yet she kept replaying the moment over and over in her thoughts. Even if there was only the tiniest chance, she figured that she had to know for certain.

Slowly, she got to her feet and began to move forward again, going further than ever before.

"My name is Stella Weaver," she announced. "Well, Estella Weaver technically, but my friends all call me Stella. Actually, anyone who doesn't want a black eye calls me Stella."

She tried to think of something else to say, of some way to make herself sound more approachable, although deep down she knew that anyone living in the tunnels would almost certainly not speak a word of English.

Yet she had to try.

"I'm an archaeologist," she continued, "which means that I'm interested in the past. Well, that's usually how it works, but sometimes the past turns out to be a little closer to the present than we ever expected. That certainly seems to be the case right now, but really all I want to do is explore the unknown. I want to understand how we, as a species, got to where we are today."

She walked on for a moment, and finally she saw that the passageway was starting to curve around to the right. She briefly considered stopping and adding this detail to her map, but she figured there was no real risk of getting lost so she continued on her way until she found several arched windows set into the wall. Walking over, she shone her flashlight through, and to her shock she found herself looking down into a huge abyss. As she adjusted the flashlight, she realized she could see more windows much further down.

"How deep *is* this place?" she whispered under her breath, before noticing that something about the light seemed different.

She switched the beam off, and now she saw that the faintest glow was flickering somewhere down near the bottom of the abyss, with its source far out of sight.

"Okay," she said out loud, trying to steady her own nerves a little, "this is... not quite what I expected, but I suppose I should have learned to expect the unexpected by now. Although I think -"

Suddenly hearing a scrabbling sound, she turned and shone the flashlight further along the passage. For a moment she spotted something moving again, far off in the shadows; the figure quickly disappeared from sight, but this time Stella was absolutely sure that it had been real.

"Hey!" she shouted, hurrying in that direction while struggling a little to stay on her feet as the ground sloped into the darkness. "I really don't want to hurt you! Can I at least see you?"

She stopped after a few more paces to lean against the wall, and as she looked at the ground she realized that if the slope became any steeper, she might actually have trouble getting back up. Part of her wanted to go back to the surface and tell her father exactly what she'd found, but at the same time she worried that he wouldn't be too impressed by vague claims of something moving in the darkness. To really get his attention, she was going to need something a little more concrete, so after a few seconds she began to carefully pick her way further down the slope.

"Do you guys have something against steps and railings?" she asked, trying to maintain a friendly tone. She spotted more text carved into the walls on either side, but in that instant she didn't really have time to stop and try to translate any of the words. "I guess you're not used to tourists, huh? When was the last time you guys even had a visitor?"

Clinging to the edge of one of the windows, she stopped and shone her flashlight ahead, only to see that the passage continue to curve down and to the right.

"I'm guessing it was a long time ago," she continued, "if it ever happened at all." Pausing, she began to realize just what those words meant. "Have you *ever* had any contact with the world up top?" she asked. "Did you ever know that there are people up there, or have you always lived down here sealed in your own little world? Then again, that wouldn't explain Monty's tomb, not unless..."

Her voice trailed off, and she realized now that she was very slowly starting to understand why the tomb was arranged in such a strange manner.

"Wow, is that possible?" she whispered. "Is that why the writing was upside-down, too?" She blinked, and in that moment she felt as if her mind might be about to break. "Is that what's been going on from the start? Is -"

Hearing a shuffling sound coming from over her shoulder, she glanced back. She assumed there'd be no sign of anyone at all, but she quickly spotted a figure standing in the shadows, having somehow double around behind her.

"Hey," she said cautiously, relieved that this figure at least hadn't immediately run away. "I'm a friend."

She began to step forward, while raising the flashlight just enough that she was finally about to see the figure's face.

"I only want to -"

Suddenly she froze, and for a few seconds she felt as if she couldn't possibly be seeing what was right in front of her. She took another step forward, making her way up the slope, and then she stopped again and stared straight ahead in incredulity until one word slipped from her lips.

"Mum?" she stammered as she saw her mother's face staring back at her. "What -"

Before she could finish, a hand touched her shoulder from behind. She spun around, and this time – as she saw a very different face glaring at her – all she could do was scream.

CHAPTER SIXTEEN

A FEW THOUSAND MILES away in Zurich, a bell briefly rang in the cool night air as a door opened and a man stepped into the bookshop.

"Good evening," August Stemmer said, looking up from the old volume he'd been examining at his desk. "I wasn't expecting anyone to call by so late."

"You're not already shut, are you?" the man said, checking his watch. "I know it's late."

"You're more than welcome to come in and take a look around," August replied, gesturing toward the book-lined aisles that led deeper into the shop. "If there's anything in particular that you want, just let me know. I try to keep things organized but sometimes people put things back on the wrong shelf." He tapped the side of his forehead. "It's all up here, though. I have something of an encyclopedic mind."

"I don't doubt that for a second," the man replied, stepping past the desk and then stopping to look along one of the aisles. "Your shop has quite the reputation. Not only in Zurich, but across the world. It's said that you have a few books here that perhaps don't exist anywhere else."

"I pride myself on that fact, Sir," August said with a faint smile, "although I should remind you that scarcity usually comes with a cost."

"Oh, I know that," the man said calmly, before heading to one of the shelves and pulling out a book. He examined the spine, before opening it to take a loot at the first few pages. "This one seems to be on the subject of werewolves."

"Lycanthropy," August said, nodding sagely. "Yes, I do rather take an interest in books on esoteric topics. Even if one doesn't believe in such things, one can learn a great deal about the people who do. They can often be far more interesting."

"You got anything on bears?"

"I'm sorry?"

"Nothing," the man replied, sliding the book back into place. "Just a little joke on my part. I heard that some people believe there are men – and women, I suppose – out there who can turn into bears."

"You'll find idiots all over the world,"

August chuckled. "If they've got money, I'm happy to sell them any of my books."

"I like your attitude," the man replied, looking along the aisle for a moment before turning to him again. "Actually, you might be able to help me after all. There *is* one particular book that I'm interested in. To be honest, it might not even exist. This is really a shot in the dark, but I figured that if there's anyone in the entire world who'd know, it'd be you."

"I'm only too happy to oblige," August said. "If I can, of course."

"It's about this civilization," the man explained, making his way back over to the desk. "An old one. An ancient one, in fact. So ancient that some people don't think it ever existed."

"The Sea Peoples?"

"No, older than that," the man countered. "Much older. We're talking about a civilization that, if it ever actually was real, would fundamentally change the way we think about the history of life on this planet." He stared at August for a moment, watching for any sign of recognition, before tilting his head slightly. "Think before the Ancient Egyptians. Before the oldest civilization currently known to man. Think about something that could forever change... everything."

"I'm sure I don't know what you mean," August said, as fear filled his bloodshot eyes and he leaned back in his chair. After a moment he got to his feet, grabbing his cane and starting to slowly make his way around from behind the desk. "As it happens, I hadn't noticed the time. I'm afraid I really must close up. I hope you won't mind coming back tomorrow if there's anything you need."

He reached for the bolt on the door, only to find that it had already been slid across. When he tried to get it open, he found that somehow it was being held firmly shut.

"I'm willing to give you the benefit of the doubt," the man behind him said. "I'm willing to accept that the book is no longer here, but I'm also fairly certain that it *was* here once. All of which leads me to wonder who you sold it to, and when, and where they might have taken it now."

"I'm sure I don't know what you're talking about," August replied, although his voice was trembling a little as he tried again and again to move the bolt. "I'm sorry, just give me a moment and I'll let you out."

"I can show myself out, thanks all the same," the man said firmly. "Just as soon as I've completed my business here. I'm afraid I might have to be a little less subtle now, Mr. Stemmer. I need the details of that book, I need to know everything about it, and I need to know tonight." He took a step forward. "A lot of lives might be on the line, including the life of a good friend who at this very moment is potentially in a lot of danger. I think -"

"Don't come any closer!" August snarled, pulling a pistol from his pocket and turning to aim it at the man's face. "I swear I'll shoot!"

"I have no doubt that you will," the man replied, keeping his eyes fixed on August and showing almost no reaction to the gun at all. "The question is, will pulling the trigger really help you all that much?"

"I am a loyal guardian of the First Order!" August screamed at the top of his voice. "I would die for the order! I don't know who you are, but you're nothing more than a pathetic little pipsqueak barking at the heels of your betters, and the First Order will crush you as it crushes all those who are deemed not worthy!"

***

As they made their way along the Limmatquai, Tomas and Barbara continued to talk about the meal they'd just enjoyed, while Tomas occasionally tried to bring up the subject of their future plans. And then, as they passed the end of a narrow alley, they both stopped as they heard a brief crashing sound coming from nearby.

"What was that?" Tomas asked cautiously.

"Probably nothing," Barbara replied, pulling on his arm gently. "Come on, let's get to the tram stop. I want to get home."

Tomas opened his mouth to reply, before hearing the sound of glass smashing.

"Someone might need help," he pointed out.

"There's nothing down there," Barbara told him. "Just some houses, and a glass shop, and an old bookshop."

"I have to check," Tomas replied, pulling away from her and starting to make his way along the alley. "Stay right there. I'm sure it's nothing but I want to make sure."

"This is nothing to do with us!" Barbara called out. "Tomas, please, it might not be safe! You don't know what you're getting yourself into!"

Picking up the pace a little, Tomas saw that the lights were still on in the little bookshop to the left. He was fairly new in Zurich, having only arrived a few months earlier, and the last thing he wanted was to get involved in a robbery when he was supposed to be enjoying his first date with Barbara from the office. At the same time, he'd grown up in a family of police officers and he felt duty-bound – even as an ordinary member of the public – to see whether he could help. Finally, as he reached the shop and looked through the window, he was about to call back to Barbara and let her know that everything was alright when suddenly an elderly man stumbled into view.

Leaning against the window, August

Stemmer placed his bloodied palms against the glass. His face had been scratched open, with something having ripped through one of his eyes and down into his cheek. For a few seconds the old man seemed to be about to call something out, until the life faded from his eyes and he slid down out of sight, leaving a bloody streak on the inside of the glass.

"Tomas, are you done?" Barbara called out from the end of the alley. "Tomas, say something! What's happening!"

For a few seconds, Tomas couldn't make sense of what he was seeing. After August had slithered down, a view of the bookshop's interior had been revealed. Tilting his head slightly, Tomas told himself that he had to be wrong, but after a few more second he realized that there was indeed a large bear sitting hunched over a desk, seemingly peering down at what appeared to be some kind of handwritten book or ledger. A moment after that the bear turned and looked at Thomas for a moment, before letting out an ear-splitting roar that shook the glass in the window.

"Run!" Tomas shouted, turning and racing back along the alley, almost colliding with Barbara as he grabbed her hand and forced her to follow him along the street. "There's a bear! We have to run!"

AMY CROSS

CHAPTER SEVENTEEN

"WHAT?"

Opening her eyes, June immediately sat up in the tent. The fabric next to her was blowing in a gentle night breeze, but June's heart was racing and after a moment she looked over at one of the other beds and saw that Stella was gone. Weaver was snoring in the bed at the far end, but as June stumbled to her feet and headed outside, she couldn't shake the feeling that something was terribly wrong.

She looked around, but there was no sign that Stella had gone to the makeshift toilet or that she was up watching the stars. At the same time, although she'd only just woken up, June couldn't help but think that she'd been disturbed by a terrible sound, by the sound of a woman screaming. No matter how hard she tried to convince herself that she was wrong and that she'd merely been troubled by an unfortunate dream, she found that she was unable to ignore the sense that the scream had come from somewhere outside her own mind, that it had reached out to her through the night air.

After waiting for a moment longer, she hurried over to the bed in the corner and reached down, shaking Weaver's shoulder until he finally rolled over and looked up at her.

"Sister June?" he said groggily. "What -"

"It's your daughter!" she gasped, unable to hide a sense of panic. "I'm sorry, I don't have time to explain right now, and I don't think I even could, but I think something has happened to Stella!"

***

"When I get my hands on that girl," Weaver said a short while later, as he and June made their way along one of the tunnels deep underground, using their flashlights to pick out the right path, "I'm going to sit her down and make her understand just how utterly selfish and wrong it is of her to go wandering off in the middle of the night."

"I don't know why she'd do such a thing," June replied.

"I do!" Weaver snapped. "She's trying to prove some kind of asinine point, either to me or to herself."

"I heard a scream coming from down here."

"You can't have done," he pointed out. "Even if someone screamed all the way down here in these tunnels, there's simply no way the sound could have traveled all the way up to the tent. It's not -"

"I'm telling you what I heard!" she snapped, turning to him as they reached the gate. "I'm sorry I don't have the logic of it all worked out, but your daughter might be in danger!"

He opened his mouth to reply to her, before freezing as he saw something dark smeared on the gate. Stepping forward, he peered more closely; when he touched the stain, he found that it was fresh blood. He stepped through and looked at the ground, and he saw more blood smeared in a path leading further down the slope.

"It's almost as if she was dragged away," June said, following him through the gate and stopping to look at the blood. "It's as if she perhaps ran this way, as if she was trying to escape from something. She got this far, she grabbed the gate, and then..."

She raised her flashlight, and sure enough she saw more smeared blood on the ground in the distance.

"And then she was pulled back down that way."

"Stella!" Weaver shouted, cupping his hands around his mouth in an effort to make himself heard properly. "Stella, where are you? Say something!"

He waited for a moment, before starting to hurry along the passage.

"Wait!" June called out, rushing after him and grabbing his arm to hold him back. "We have no idea what's going on here, but I really don't think we should simply go charging in like this."

"I have to find my daughter!" he spluttered.

"I know, but -"

"I'm not leaving her!" he shouted, pulling away and setting off again. "I'm not going to make the same mistake I made with my wife!"

"With your..."

June hesitated for a moment, before hurrying after him again. This time, instead of trying to grab his arm and hold him back, she settled for keeping pace with him as they made their way further and further along the sloping passageway.

"We won't help Stella if we go blundering into this mess," she pointed out. "That might very well be how she ended up in this trouble in the first place. I really think that calmer heads should prevail in a situation such as this, and just a moment of contemplation and planning might really do us no end of good."

"That's easy for you to say," he replied,

already sounding more than a little out of breath. "Stay back and think about things all you want, Sister June, but I'm going to find my daughter!"

"We both want the same thing," she told him, before stopping as she spotted what appeared to be some arched windows at the side of the passage. "Wait one moment," she added, making her way over and looking through to see the vast abyss stretching out deep below. "Doctor Weaver, I rather fear that our search radius just became significantly larger."

"I don't have time for that right now!" he yelled, already hurrying off into the distance. "I have to find my daughter!"

June began to turn to follow him, but at the last second she found herself once more looking into the abyss. She saw more arched windows far below, suggesting that the passages extended deeper underground, but for a few seconds she could only stare at the strange scene as she felt a tingling sense of familiarity starting to wriggle its way through her chest.

"I've seen this before," she whispered finally. "I don't know where, but... I've seen this place before."

She hesitated, and then – realizing that she mustn't let Weaver get too far ahead – she turned once again to go after him. Before she could take even one more step, however, she spotted an open doorway on the passage's opposite wall; she felt sure that the doorway hadn't been there before, yet now she felt almost as if she was being called by some hidden force to go and take a look.

"Stella!" Weaver shouted in the distance. "If you can hear me, say something! Stella, where are you?"

"Hello?" June said cautiously, stepping slowly toward the doorway. "Is... is there somebody in there?"

As she took another step forward, she felt as if she could hear a faint whispering voice coming from somewhere nearby, staying just far enough away for its words to remain muddled. Although she could feel a growing twist of fear in her chest, June approached the door and looked through at the darkness, and then – with a trembling hand – she slowly raised her flashlight.

She stopped as soon as she saw the white tiled floor of the next room. Furrowing her brow, she realized that this tiled floor seemed strangely familiar, although she quickly told herself that this was impossible. Nevertheless, she had to take a few seconds to regather her courage before she tilted the flashlight's beam a little more, and then she let out a gasp as she saw not only a small table but also the foot of a large staircase.

"This can't be," she whispered, trying to steady her nerves. "It's simply impossible..."

Stepping through the doorway, she felt her feet move from the rocky ground of the passage to the tiled floor of the large open hallway. Ahead, moonlight was streaming through a window that she remembered all too well, even if she knew there was no way it could possibly exist beneath the Sahara. She aimed the flashlight all around, trying to find some proof that she was wrong, yet with each and every passing second she felt more and more certain that she was back in the one place she'd always sworn to stay away from forever. Even the smell was starting to seem familiar, as she picked up the scent of so much mahogany furniture.

"This isn't possible," she said firmly, with a hint of anger in her voice as tears began to fill her eyes. "Holdham Hall is thousand of miles away, it's in England, it's not buried under the desert here in Africa. It can't be, it -"

Suddenly hearing footsteps, she turned and aimed her flashlight up at the side of the staircase. To her shock, a young girl hurried into view and dropped to her knees, smiling as she peered between the railings.

"Hello," the girl said brightly. "Who are you?"

"This is impossible," June said as she stared back up into the girl's eyes. "I... I'm you!"

AMY CROSS

CHAPTER EIGHTEEN

"BUT IF YOU'RE ME," the little girl said, as she got to her feet and hurried down the stairs, stopping at the bottom and looking at June again, "then who am *I*?"

"What kind of trickery is this?" June whispered. "What cruelty?"

"You're funny," the girl replied, keeping her eyes fixed on June. "I know it's late and I shouldn't be up, but I heard the knocking again and... well, Miss Bridger never likes it when I talk about such things, but I simply know that something's wrong. I hate being a little girl, it means no-one ever believes you when you tell them something."

"I can't be here," June said, taking a step back. "This is wrong."

"Can you help me?" the girl asked, reaching

toward her with an outstretched hand. "Please? It's so cold and dark, and I know I'm being naughty but I'm convinced that something's down here."

"I can't be here," June said again, before turning to head back through the doorway. "I'm not -"

Stopping suddenly, she heard a knocking sound in the distance. She told herself that she mustn't overreact, that she was merely experiencing some kind of vision of Holdham Hall, that the real place was so very far away, yet as the knocking continued she was drawn back to the days many years earlier when she'd been a terrified little girl in a very large and spooky old English school. She swallowed hard, still hoping to break the spell and find herself back in the underground tunnels beneath the Sahara, but as the knocking continued she slowly turned to see the image of herself still standing nearby.

"Can you hear it too?" the little girl asked, with tears in her eyes. "Please tell me you can hear it too..."

"There's no need to be afraid," June told her, although she knew she didn't sound very convincing. "You should go back to bed with the other girls."

"What do you think it wants?" the girl replied.

"I think that doesn't matter and it's none of

our business," June said firmly. "You don't need to go rushing around, poking your nose into these things. Just -"

"I'm going to find out!" the girl said, turning and racing through to the dining room.

"No, wait!" June shouted, but the girl was already out of sight. "Don't do this," she continued, and now she too had tears in her eyes. "It won't end well. You'll never get over it, and poor Meredith..."

Her voice trailed off, and now the hall was silent again. Although she knew she should simply walk away, June couldn't help but remember all the pain and fear of Holdham Hall, and now she found herself wondering whether perhaps – by some miracle – she might be able to undo all the horrors that had taken place when she was younger.

A moment later she heard the knocking sound again.

"Wait!" she shouted, hurrying past the foot of the stairs. "Come back! You have no idea what you're getting yourself involved with!"

***

As soon as she reached the dining room, June stopped as she felt the past flooding back. She'd spent so long deliberately trying to forget about Holdham Hall, and eventually she'd been able to focus on the present and the future, but now she realized that all the memories had been lurking in her mind the whole time, waiting for the moment when they could return.

That moment had arrived.

The dining room was as large and gloomy as she remembered, with six tall windows on one side letting moonlight stream through onto the long table where all the girls used to eat. Stepping over to the head of the table, June looked at the particular chair where she'd always sat; Miss Bridger always wanted the girls to sit in the same seats for every meal, and June had enjoyed her spot right next to dear Meredith. Now, as she looked at the next seat along, she found herself thinking about Meredith's final moments, about that awful night when everything had gone so terribly wrong and the spectral figure had got what it wanted.

"Meredith," she whispered now, as if she half-expected to see the ghostly little girl appear in the chair. "I'm so sorry. I wish -"

Hearing a scratching sound, she realized that something was under the table. She crouched down and immediately saw herself as a young girl hiding between the chairs.

"It's here," the girl whispered, her voice tense with fear. "I know you heard it."

"No good can come of acting in this manner," June told her. "Please, come out and go back to the dormitory."

"But it's here!" the girl hissed. "The ghost! I know you saw it too!"

"Of course I saw it too," June replied, trying to avoid sounding too exasperated. "If you saw it, then obviously I saw it as well, because I'm you!"

"Then you know," the girl pointed out. "If you know, why are you trying to deny it?"

"Because this is the past," June told her, "and the past should stay buried."

"Am I buried?" the girl asked. "*Should* I be buried?"

"I have to find Stella."

"You have to help me."

"You can't be helped!" June snapped, before taking a deep breath. "There's nothing I can do about any of this, because it all happened so very long ago. It happened before everything else, and there's nothing whatsoever that can be done to fix the tragedy."

"You still have to try, though," the girl replied. "Don't you?"

June opened her mouth to reply, but in that moment she heard footsteps out in the hall. She hesitated, fully aware that the footsteps had to be in her mind, but finally pure fear took over and she crawled under the table, joining the little girl between the chair-legs.

"I wish Meredith was here," the girl said.

"Meredith is long gone," June replied, as a

flicker of fear moved up her spine.

"Where do you think she's gone?"

"Will you stop asking so many questions," June replied, turning to look toward the doorway. "There's really no -"

She froze as she saw someone walking into the dining room. She could only see the bottom half of the person's legs, of course, as they moved slowly past the table. Unable to look away, June watched as the strange figure made its way through the moonlit room, finally stopping at the far end of the table.

"I think she knows we're here," the little girl whispered. "Of course, when this really happened, it wasn't you and me, was it? I was here, but I was with -"

"Meredith," June replied, still struggling to hold back the worst memories of that night.

"And what happened to Meredith?"

"I don't want to think about it," June said firmly, still watching the feet of the figure at the head of the table.

"But you must," the girl pointed out, as her voice began to change, becoming a little higher. "You remember *me*, June, don't you? Please, tell me you haven't forgotten me."

"Don't be silly," June replied, turning to her. "I could never -"

In that moment she saw an entirely different

face staring back at her. She almost screamed, but she managed to stay quiet as she found herself staring at the one face she'd tried to forget for so very long.

"That's better," Meredith said with a faint smile. "I know you hadn't forgotten me, not really. And now here you are, underground in the Sahara, and I've come back to you. It's strange, isn't it? I really shouldn't be here, but then none of this should be here. You're not actually in Holdham Hall, June. You're still in that strange maze of tunnels, you're still supposed to be looking for Stella. You realize that, don't you?"

"I don't understand any of this," June replied, as a tear ran down her cheek.

"Then try a little harder," Meredith said firmly. "Use that brain of yours that got you out of those other scrapes. You're not an idiot, June, and I know you pay attention. Why are you here, anyway? I know this place is where you experienced your greatest moment of fear, but it'd be far more useful if you imagined the convent instead." She paused, as a cracking sound began to break out under the skin of her face, and as shards of glass started to poke out through bloodied cuts. "Don't you remember the painting?"

"What painting?" June asked, as she watched a larger glass shard cutting its way out from beneath Meredith's left cheek. "Wait, what are you doing? Stop!"

"You know where this place really is!" Meredith gasped, as yet more glass began to cut her tongue. "Why are you using one fear to bury another?"

"I'm not!" June screamed. "Stop! Leave me -"

CHAPTER NINETEEN

"- ALONE!"

Leaning forward, June placed her hands on the rough, rocky floor of the cavern. Her flashlight lay nearby, its beam shining directly at her hands, and after a moment June looked around and realized that she was back in the underground complex beneath the Sahara. The vision of Holdham Hall had vanished, as had the awful sight of Meredith reliving the moment of her death.

Grabbing the flashlight, June scrambled back out of the cavern and into the sloping corridor before there could be any risk of Holdham Hall or Meredith returning.

A moment later, hearing voices up ahead, she looked down the slope. Weaver was somewhere nearby, speaking angrily to someone. June got to her feet and brushed some dust from herself, and then she tried to pull her thoughts together as she made her way to another door. Meredith's words were still ringing in her mind as she reached the doorway, but when she looked into another room she saw that Weaver was pacing back and forth in some kind of jungle while a woman stood watching nearby.

"None of this makes a damn bit of sense," Weaver muttered, clearly frustrated as he stopped and turned to look at the woman. "How can you be sick now? Don't you have any idea how important my work is, Gretchen?"

"I'm sorry," the woman replied, "it's not like I chose for this to happen. I just think that I need to get back and see a doctor, just in case there's something wrong."

"That would add weeks to our project," Weaver told her with a sigh. "Weeks! Woman, do you have any idea what that would mean? My funding would run out and everything I've worked toward would be for nothing. I'd never be able to get the board to give me another chance!"

"I know," the woman said, shaking her head. She paused for a moment, before touching her wrist as if she was checking her own pulse. "Believe me, Morty, I'm more than aware of the importance of your work. I've always tried to support you, and I still want to do that, it's just that I'm not feeling well and I'm scared that... well, you know what I'm scared of. I think I need to see a doctor."

"Who is this?" June asked, stepping through the doorway. "What -"

Before she could finish, she felt her feet starting to sink into some soft ground. Looking down, she saw that she was standing on the forest floor; when she looked up, she saw daylight streaming between the thick canopy of the jungle high above. The image, some kind of mirage, was as complete and as convincing as the facsimile of Holdham Hall, and after a few seconds she realized she could even feel the intense humidity in the air all around.

"What are you doing here?" Weaver asked, turning to her.

"Whatever this is," June replied, "it's not real."

"What are you talking about?" he snapped, before wiping some sweat from his brow. "I'm sorry, Sister June, you've arrived at a rather inopportune moment. We're months into this project, we're on the verge of making a breakthrough, and my wife has chosen this moment to tell me that she's coming down with symptoms of one thing or another."

"I might be wrong," the woman said, although the fear in her voice suggested that she didn't really believe a word that was coming from her own mouth. "It's possible. I just want to get myself checked for certain, that's all. If it's malaria -"

"You haven't got malaria!" Weaver said angrily.

"That's what she died of," June whispered. "Stella told me."

"I just need more time!" Weaver continued, turning and pacing back over toward a nearby tree before turning again. "Another week or two, that's all I'm asking for, Gretchen!"

"Fine," the woman replied. "You know what? I'm sure you're right. Mum's always been a hypochondriac and I suppose I'm just following suit." She forced a somewhat unconvincing smile. "I'm sorry, Morty, just ignore me, I'm being an idiot and we need to get on with the project. I'm sure I'll feel better in a day or two."

"You're just adjusting to the jungle," he told her. "That's all."

"I know," she said, stepping over to him and kissing him on the cheek, then walking past and picking her way between two trees. "I'm going to check those other traps. I think I missed two, and you never know, we could be in luck."

"Yes, do that," Weaver said, as he wiped yet more sweat from his brow. "I'll be with you presently."

June watched as the woman walked away,

and then she headed over to Weaver. She knew that the jungle scene couldn't possibly be real, but she was starting to worry that just as she'd experienced a vision of her moment of greatest fear, Weaver now seemed to be lost in his own personal nightmare. Reaching out, she touched the side of his arm.

"Doctor Weaver," she said, "I need you to listen to me very carefully. This jungle, the vision of your wife... none of it's real."

"What?" he replied, turning to her. "What are you talking about?"

"Look at me," she continued, "and remember why I'm here. I'm here because I came to your dig site in the Sahara. You're there with your daughter Stella, and she's missing and we have to find her. This jungle scene is just something from your past, it's possibly your greatest fear or something like that, and you're reliving it." She looked around, feeling increasingly puzzled by what she was seeing. "And I'm reliving it with you, apparently," she added. "That's rather odd. It's one thing for a person to hallucinate, but it's quite another if others are able to see the same thing."

"What are you nattering on about now?" Weaver asked.

"Whatever happened here," June said, seeing the fear in his eyes, "whatever fear or horror you're reliving, you have to understand that it's not really happening. Not right here, at least. It might have happened similarly in the past, but right here and right now the priority has to be finding Stella."

"I -"

Weaver hesitated; his usual bluster was gone, and he seemed to be on the verge of understanding exactly what June meant.

"Stella's missing," June reminded him. "In the tunnels. Under the Sahara. We have to find her."

"Yes," he replied, as if he was emerging from a daze. "Of course we do. I'm sorry, I don't know what happened, I think I just allowed myself to become distracted." He turned and hurried toward the doorway. "We must find Stella immediately, she -"

"Morty?"

He stopped in the doorway, and June turned to see that his wife was making her way back to the clearing.

"Morty," the woman continued, "I don't know how to tell you this, but there's something I've been keeping from you. I don't want you to get angry, but I'm not feeling too great and I'm wondering whether I should maybe see a doctor."

"It's on a loop," June whispered.

"What was that?" Weaver asked, turning to look back toward his wife again. "Gretchen, what did you just say?"

"I know the timing's lousy," the woman said, stopping and rubbing the back of her neck, "but there are just a few too many symptoms for me to ignore. They've been building for a few days now and I hate to do this, but would you mind terribly if I went back to the village and tried to arrange to see a doctor? I'm worried... I know you'll think I'm being silly, but I just can't shake this silly fear that it might be malaria."

"Malaria?" Weaver replied, furrowing his brow. "Gretchen, you haven't got malaria! For God's sake, woman, why are you coming out with this claptrap now of all times? Have you got any idea how close I am to finding those ruins? There's no way you can go back alone, I'd have to go with you, and then there wouldn't be time to get here again during this season! All my work would be for nothing!"

"I know," she said with a sigh, "which is why I waited so long to bring this up, but something just isn't right with me. And I know you think I probably can't turn back by myself, but I think I probably could."

"But I need you here!" he said firmly.

"You've done this part already," June reminded him. "Doctor Weaver, listen to me, you need to break out of this and come with me, we have to go and find Stella before it's too late!"

"Stella?" He turned to June. "Stella's back at the boarding school in England. She's not here, we wouldn't bring a child to the jungle. Are you crazy?"

"No, Stella's a grown woman and she's lost in the tunnels," June said firmly. "All of this, with your wife, happened a long time ago. Doctor Weaver, please, you have to listen very carefully to what I'm telling you! Time's running out and you have to break free from this fantasy so we can find your daughter!"

CHAPTER TWENTY

"REMARKABLE!" WEAVER GASPED AS he and June stepped back out into the sloping passageway. Already, the doorway in front of them had faded to darkness, and when he shone his flashlight back through he saw only another rocky chamber. "It seemed so real while I was in there."

He stepped forward, as if he was going to go back through, but June grabbed him by the arm and held him in place.

"I just want to see one more time," he protested. "For curiosity."

"I rather fear that you'd be trapped again," June told him. "Although I have to admit, you didn't put up too much of a fight in the end. Persuading you to come out was a lot easier than I thought it might be." She furrowed her brow. "Easier than I found it, at least."

"I hear her!" he said suddenly, turning and looking along the passageway, then making his way deeper while aiming his flashlight straight ahead. "Sister June, I think I can hear Stella's voice!"

June opened her mouth to reply, but at the last moment she realized that he might be right. A woman was talking somewhere in the distance, and as she set off after Weaver she began to realized that she too could hear Stella speaking to someone, although as she reached yet another doorway she noticed that the voice sounded calm and happy, almost as if -

Stopping next to Weaver, she looked into another chamber and saw that Stella was on the floor, kneeling by a chair with her head resting on the lap of a familiar woman. A moment later the woman turned to look down at Stella, and June realized that this was once again Weaver's wife Gretchen.

"You again?" Weaver snapped, stepping forward. "I don't know what you are, but you're not real! My wife is dead!"

"It's not her," June reminded him. "It's not even the same illusion you saw in the jungle just now, at least I don't think it is. That was *your* vision of your wife. This is Stella's vision, and they're probably quite different."

"I've missed you so much, Mummy," Stella

said, as Gretchen stroked the top of her head. "I never thought I'd get another chance to talk to you."

"Well, I'm here now," Gretchen replied with a smile.

"What in the name of all that's holy is going on?" Weaver whispered.

"I'm not quite sure," June replied, as they both watched the strangely peaceful scene. "I thought this place presented you with your worst nightmares and fears, but Stella..." Her voice trailed off for a moment as she saw that Stella's face was covered in scratches, while blood stained the side of her shirt. "This doesn't seem much like a nightmare to me," she continued. "It seems more like some kind of strange wish fulfillment."

"Have you been watching me?" Stella asked, sniffing back more tears as she clung to her mother's lap. "Have you seen how hard I've worked? I did it all for you, Mummy. I kept telling myself that you were watching over me, and that you'd be proud of me." She paused again, as if she was scared to go on. "*Are* you proud?" she added finally, and now the fear was evident in her trembling voice. "Am I doing enough?"

"Proud of you?" Gretchen replied, as if she was genuinely shocked by the question. "Am I proud of you? Oh you poor, silly girl, how could you even think to ask such a question?" She stroked her daughter's hair for a few more seconds, before her hand fell still. "Of course I'm not proud of you," she added through gritted teeth. "How could I possibly be proud of such a pathetic, miserable failure? You're nothing but a foolish little clone of your disgusting father."

"You don't mean that," Stella said, looking up at her. "Please, Mummy, tell me you don't mean that."

"I mean every word," Gretchen sneered. "If you'd possessed even an ounce of intelligence in your life, you'd have realized that long ago. You're nothing but a moronic little child who couldn't carve her own way through life and instead had to slavishly copy her idiotic father. How could you think that any mother would ever be proud of that? How could you think that any mother would ever love you?"

"Why are you saying that?" Stella whimpered, as fresh tears ran down her face. "Mummy -"

"I don't want anything to do with you," Gretchen said, placing a hand against her face and starting to push her away. "I wouldn't if I was alive, and now that I'm dead I certainly don't see why I should waste my time."

"Mummy, no!" Stella sobbed.

"We're getting out of here," Weaver said, rushing over to his daughter and grabbing her from behind, then starting to drag her toward the door.

"Sister June, can you help me? I can't let her listen to this nonsense for a moment longer!"

June hurried up behind Stella and took hold of one of her arms, and together she and Weaver pulled her toward the door as the ghostly figure of Gretchen Weaver slowly got to her feet and began to follow.

"Look at you now," Gretchen snarled. "There's no point to you, Stella. You're such a terrible disappointment."

"No, I can change!" Stella gasped, breaking free from Weaver and Sister June and rushing forward, dropping to her knees in front of Gretchen and grabbing her legs so that she could hug her tight. "Tell me what to do and I'll do it! I won't stop at anything, Mummy!" After a moment she pulled back and looked up at her. "I know you died too young, I know you should have had many more years. I know you should have made it out of that jungle, but..."

Her voice trailed off for a few seconds, and then she slowly turned and glared angrily at her father.

"But you killed her!" she snapped.

"This is all getting too intense," Sister June said uncomfortably. "I think -"

"You murdered her!" Stella screamed, pointing at Weaver. "Admit it! You knew she was sick but you wouldn't let her turn back and see a doctor! You only cared about your precious study and those ruins, so you forced Mum to keep going even though she was showing the earliest signs of malaria!"

"Stella," Weaver replied, "I -"

"She could have survived," Stella continued breathlessly. "She probably would have survived if you hadn't made her stay by your side until she couldn't even walk! It was your greed and vanity that killed her!"

"You don't know what you're saying," June told her. "Listen to me, this isn't real, this is all an illusion that has been designed somehow to play on your worst fears."

"Ask him!" Stella shouted, still pointing at her father. "Make him tell the truth! After all these years, make him admit what he did!"

"I think we're each being tested," June explained. "Your father and I managed to break out of our own illusions, and now you have to do the same. Stella, I know it's hard and I know this must hurt so very much, but we have to get you out of here and make our way back up to the surface, and then we have to try to get away from here. Do you understand?" She held a hand out toward the younger woman. "Please, Stella," she added. "I understand how awful this is, but for one moment can't you trust me?"

"I'm not going anywhere until he admits

what he did to my mother!" Stella replied, clinging tighter and tighter to Gretchen's legs. "Make him do it, Mummy! Make him tell the truth!"

"Perhaps we have to try this another way," June muttered, before stepping forward. "Stella -"

"No," Weaver said suddenly, grabbing her arm from behind. "Sister June, please, you don't realize what's happening here."

She turned to him.

"Follow me," he continued, pulling her through the doorway and back out into the passageway.

"We can't just leave her in there!" June insisted.

"We're not," he replied, and then they both turned to see that the room was empty again. Weaver aimed his flashlight through the doorway, and the beam picked out nothing but the rocky ground. "That wasn't her fear, Sister June," he continued. "It was still mine. I suppose I hadn't left it behind in that other room the way I thought I had."

"I don't understand," June stammered, staring into the room for a moment before turning to him again. "If that was *your* fear, then..."

"My greatest fear," he explained, "wasn't facing Gretchen's death again. It was Stella finding out that her mother died because I wouldn't let her go to the doctor when her symptoms first showed.

Everything that was said just now in those two rooms was completely true. I can never forgive myself, but truly my greatest fear has always been that Stella might learn the truth. If she knew that I was responsible for her mother's death, I don't think she'd ever look at me again."

June opened her mouth to reply, but for a few seconds she had no idea what to say. A moment later, however, they both turned as they heard footsteps racing closer through the darkness, and finally a bloodied and wounded Stella stumbled into view.

"Run!" she screamed frantically. "Get out of here! Both of you! You have to run!"

CHAPTER TWENTY-ONE

"THAT'S RIGHT," WEAVER SAID a short while later, as he helped his daughter off the top of the ladder and back into the camp on the surface. "Take your time. Make sure you don't trip."

"I'm fine!" Stella hissed, reaching out to support herself against some nearby rocks. "Make sure Sister June gets up."

Weaver reached down and helped June, who'd insisted on making sure that Stella got to safety first. Finally, once they were all out, Weaver turned and looked back into the hole, but to his relief he still saw no sign that they were being followed.

"Do you see anything?" Stella gasped breathlessly.

"No," he replied, before turning to her.

"What *should* I see?"

"There are these things down there," she told him, her eyes wide with fear. "I don't know exactly what they are. One attacked me, then two more came, then more until I could feel their scratchy little hands all over me. They were hissing and laughing, trying to drag me deeper and deeper down into that place. Eventually I managed to fight back. There might have been a lot of them, but they weren't very strong and once they realized I could hurt them, they weren't quite so brave." She paused for a moment. "I don't know what they were, Dad, but I don't think they were human."

"They were probably a figment of your imagination," he told her, although his voice betrayed a certain hint of caution. "Sister June and I experienced something similar, a kind of hallucination that -"

"Do these look like hallucinations?" she asked, holding up her arms to reveal thick cuts that had – in places – torn her flesh to ribbons.

"No," Weaver stammered, clearly a little lost for words, "but -"

"I had my hallucinations down there," she continued through gritted teeth. "These creatures were different. I don't know what they were, but they were definitely real."

"Sister June, what's your opinion?" Weaver asked, turning to see that she was sitting nearby with a strange faraway look in her eyes as she stared out toward the horizon. He waited for a moment, before stepping toward her. "Sister June? Are you alright?"

"I'm quite unharmed, thank you," she replied as if she was emerging from a daze. "It's just that I was rather struck by something unusual while I was down there." She looked up at him. "When I looked down into the depths of that abyss, I don't know how but in some way I... recognized what I saw."

"How's that possible?" Weaver asked.

"I have no idea," she admitted, "but the sensation is very strong. Somehow, somewhere, I've seen that place before. Or if not that place, then something very much like it. I just can't quite remember how."

Weaver opened his mouth to reply, before turning and heading back over to his daughter. He reached down and put a hand on her shoulder, and then – as the wind picked up a little more – he looked over and saw that the tent was struggling against the elements.

"We have to get out of here, Dad," Stella said after a few seconds.

"I don't think that's an option tonight," Weaver replied as he looked toward the horizon. In the darkness, he could just about make out a line of bad weather moving closer. "There's a sandstorm picking up."

"Are you kidding?" Stella snapped, getting to her feet and following his gaze. "How is this possible? How could the timing be so bad? It can't be a coincidence."

"Sandstorms are quite common at this time of -"

"Dad, this is too convenient," she said firmly. "It's almost as if someone's causing it on purpose to keep us here."

"That's impossible," he replied. "Stella, I know you've been through quite a bad ordeal, but you mustn't let go of logic and reason. The factors that cause sandstorms are far too numerous to be controlled by any man. This is simply, as I'm sure you'll understand, an unfortunate coincidence." He looked toward the horizon again. "It's shaping up to be a big one, too. I don't think we have any chance of getting away before tomorrow morning at the earliest, so I'm going to focus on battening down the hatches." He turned and shuffled past her. "I'll do it all. You must rest."

Stella sighed, but as the side of the tent started flapping in the wind she picked her way over to the spot where Sister June was still sitting alone.

"I don't buy it," Stella muttered. "We've gone weeks without a sandstorm. Am I supposed to believe that one's just conveniently showing up right when we want to get out of here?" She rubbed the side of her head. "Then again, Dad's right, there's no way anyone could cause one to happen. I don't know what's going on, but I feel like I'm starting to lose my goddamn mind."

Realizing that June hadn't replied, she looked down to see that she was still lost in thought.

"What did you see, Sister June?" she asked. "Did you hallucinate something bad down there?"

"I... had a certain experience," June replied, "but that's really not what's causing me so much concern. I've never been to Africa before, so there's really no way that I could ever have seen what's down in that place, yet something about it seemed so utterly familiar. I'm trying to work out how, but for whatever reason the truth just won't come to me. I'm rather afraid that I'm somehow subconsciously blocking it all out, perhaps because the truth is too horrific to accept."

Stella paused, before taking a seat next to her.

"I relieved the night my mother died," she said after a moment. "Well, not the actual night she died, but the night I heard about it. I was at the boarding school and the headmistress sent for me after lights out. I stood in her study while she explained that Mum had died of malaria, and that Dad would be home shortly, and she told me that I had to be a good brave little girl and not cry or make a fuss." She swallowed hard. "I wasn't even supposed to tell the other girls that Mum had died. I was supposed to just carry on as normal, which I did. And then down there, in those caves or whatever they are, I had to relive that moment over and over again. That sensation of the bottom falling out of my world was just going round and round, and I felt like it was never going to end."

"I'm sorry you had to experience that," June told her.

"I realized it was an illusion pretty quickly."

"I mean the first time it happened," June replied, reaching over and squeezing her hand. "I know what it's like to be at one of those schools. I also know what it's like to..."

Her voice trailed off, and after a moment she pulled her hand back.

"Well," she added, forcing a smile, "I don't suppose there's any point digging into it so much. I'm glad you were able to separate fantasy from reality down there, though. I think your father and I found the task a little more difficult."

"Those creatures were real," Stella said firmly, before looking over at the hole that led underground. "I know Dad still doesn't quite believe me, but I swear they're down there. What if they come up and try to get us?"

"Our one advantage," June replied, "seems to be that they're extremely cautious, at least when they don't have a numerical advantage. Even then, you said that they withdrew once you began to fight back. I have a sneaking suspicion that they rely upon other tricks to subdue their prey."

"I don't know what the hell kind of place we've uncovered down there," Stella murmured, "but I want it dug out and examined, and I want to personally be in charge of dissecting one of those little bastards. I know this might sound crazy, Sister June, but when I was down there it was like some kind of vision of a nightmare world. It actually reminded me of some paintings I saw when I was a kid. I don't ever want to go down there again, at least not without some proper weapons."

June opened her mouth to reply, before hesitating as Stella's words sank in a little more. She told herself that she had to be wrong, but now her memories were clearing and she was starting to understand just where she'd seen that strange underground world before.

"No," she whispered, "it's not possible."

"Hmm?" Stella replied, watching the hole for a moment longer before turning to her. "What's not possible? Sister June, hey, you look a little pale suddenly. What -"

"Father, help us!" June gasped, dropping down onto her knees and clasping her hands together tight in prayer. "It cannot be! Father, please, reveal the truth, because if it's what I think it is down there, the end of days must be upon us!"

"Sister June, you're freaking me out," Stella said, staring at her with an expression of shock. "What's going on?"

"That place," June replied, keeping her hands together in prayer as she turned to her. "I know where I've seen it before! I know why it looks so horrifically familiar!"

CHAPTER TWENTY-TWO

"WELL," SISTER BONNIE SAID with a sigh as she set the pair of secateurs down on the desk, "who knew that a chrysanthemum competition could get so heated. And controversial."

She wiped some sweat from her brow.

"And violent."

"Sister June is usually in charge of this sort of thing," Sister Agnes said as she made her way into the room and placed the petty cash tin on one of the shelves. "I must confess, until today I had no idea just how much work she must put in when it comes to these events. She always makes it look so easy, and yet -"

Before she could finish, they both heard the grandfather clock chiming in the hallway.

"Midnight," Sister Bonnie said, rolling her

eyes. "I must admit, this has been the most challenging day I have ever experienced at St. Jude's. I know I probably shouldn't say this, but I really do hope that Sister June returns soon to take over these duties again. Do you happen to remember when she's due back?"

"I believe she said she might be a week or more."

"And where exactly did she go?"

"I think she said something about Africa."

"You know," Sister Bonnie continued, "I shouldn't gossip, but there's sometimes something a little odd about Sister June. She just seems rather nervous most of the time, especially when the phone rings. If I didn't know better, I'd be tempted to think that she's hiding from something."

"I've heard some rather odd stories," Sister Agnes confessed.

"Really?" Sister Bonnie stepped closer. "Such as?"

"Just whispers here and there, little suggestions that sometimes Sister June is called away to work for..." Sister Agnes glanced around, as if she was worried that they might be overheard. "I suppose that's the problem," she added with a sigh. "Nobody knows, but she's always granted these leaves of absence, even at the shortest possible notice. It's as if somebody higher up in the chain of command reaches out and makes sure that she's available."

"Why would that be?"

"I have no idea." Sister Agnes glanced around again. "Then there are the rumors about something very odd that's supposed to have happened here back in the 1960s. Have you ever heard anyone talk about Sister Rose or Sister Vanessa?"

"Those names seem a little familiar."

"I believe it was all covered up," Sister Agnes explained, "and I'm sure we shouldn't be digging into it now. But something happened here, and from what I can tell Sister June was right in the middle of it all. Then again, Sister June seems to be a magnet for such things. I'm not the only one who's noticed that, either. She just seems to attract trouble. Why, there was even talk back in the 1960s of a bear being seen in the garden, although I can't quite bring myself to believe such errant nonsense." She looked down at the secateurs again. "But I suppose she *does* know how to organize a chrysanthemum competition."

"I couldn't believe it when Phyllis Walton threw those secateurs at Molly Ringhorne," Sister Bonnie said, "or when the wretched things became so deeply embedded in the wall. Phyllis has a really strong throwing arm. Must be all those lawn bowls tournaments."

Hearing a bumping sound coming from far

off in the convent, they both turned to look back toward the doorway.

"I rather think we shouldn't stay up gossiping like this," Sister Agnes said with a firm nod. "Sister Bonnie, we must attend to our nightly duties and then I rather think it's beyond time for us both to retire for the night. I don't know about you, but I have to cover for more of Sister June's duties in the morning. I think I need a very good night's sleep."

***

Once she had made sure that the petty cash was secured in the safe, Sister Agnes made a point of walking from room to room, checking that nothing was amiss before she retired for the night. This wasn't one of her duties, of course, but she always liked to be extra certain that the convent was in good order.

Reaching the hallway again, she stopped as she heard footsteps. She turned to look at another door, just as Sister Bonnie backed her way slowly out from one of the other rooms.

"Sister Bonnie, what -"

In that instant, Sister Bonnie screamed and spun round, staring at Sister Agnes with an expression of wide-eyed horror.

"Sister Bonnie, are you quite alright?" Sister

Agnes asked. "What are you doing creeping around at such a late hour? I thought you'd gone upstairs."

"I was going to," Sister Bonnie stammered, "but then I thought I heard a noise and I went to investigate. I didn't find anything, though, so I suppose I was just getting a little jumpy over nothing." She paused, before looking over her shoulder. "You're going to think that I'm a terrible fool," she continued, "and you'd be right, but in truth I sometimes find the convent to be a little... spooky."

"Spooky?"

"At night, I mean," Sister Bonnie continued, turning to her again. "I know the Lord wouldn't allow anything bad to happen here. It's just this weird feeling I can't shake."

"I fully understand," Sister Agnes said as she led her across the hallway. Together, they began to make their way up the stairs. "This isn't something that one can discuss with most of the others, for they tend to dislike such talk, but St. Jude's is certainly an old building that seems to have a great deal of history. Indeed, sometimes I find myself quite taken aback by the design of the place."

Stopping for a moment, they both looked up at a huge painting that hung over the staircase. A chaotic clash of oil-painted colors, the painting showed sections of ravaged buildings rising up from a miasma of heat and fire; in some places the buildings seemed to be collapsed into the inferno, while in others tiny figures clung to the disintegrating stones as they tried desperately to keep from falling. Measuring a good thirty feet by twenty, the painting had long dominated the hallway and landing at St. Jude's, and new nuns were often asked to study the imagery and write about its inferred meaning.

"Take this," Sister Agnes continued. "Do you know the title?"

"Of course," Sister Bonnie replied. "*The Flames Shall Swallow Them All*, by the great nineteenth century artist Anthony Toyner. It was one of his earlier masterpieces, was it not?"

"My art history is rather poor, I'm afraid," Sister Agnes muttered. "How can any place be considered peaceful when it is faced every day with this... monstrosity? I know that some of the nuns went to Sister Margaret many years ago and implored her to have it taken down, but she insisted that it should remain as a reminder of what happens to those who sin. Her successors have taken the same attitude, even I'm sure that if a vote were to be carried out in the convent, the nuns would overwhelmingly opt to have it moved out of sight."

"I wouldn't mind holding that vote."

"Others have tried."

"And failed?"

"One does not get very far in this convent by challenging authority. This painting is a perfect example. You must be more like the rest of us, and simply try to ignore that it's here. I find that unless my attention is specifically directed to the image, I am often quite able to pretend that it doesn't exist at all."

"And what exactly does it show?" Sister Bonnie asked, tilting her head slightly as she continued to stare up at the painting. "I've heard many theories."

"As have I, but the most common is that Mr. Toyner suffered an uncharacteristic fit of hysteria one night, possibly after drinking too much. Apparently he tried to disown the painting after, even going so far as to deny that he'd even painted it. The canvas was saved from a rubbish pile, but Toyner threatened legal action against anyone who even mentioned it in the same breath as his name." She paused for a few seconds, admiring the brushwork even as she saw the image of windows overlooking the flames. "I shouldn't think that I blame him for that," she added. "Who would ever want to be credited with the production of such a monstrous vision?"

"I quite agree," Sister Bonnie replied. "I'm not sure I should look at it much longer. I rather fear that it might give me bad dreams."

"Then we must go to our rooms," Sister

Agnes told her, as they proceeded on their way. "Let us think no more of Mr. Toyner, or of his hideous painting of the fires of Hell."

CHAPTER TWENTY-THREE

"WHAT DID YOU JUST say?" Stella asked, staring in shock at the side of Sister June's face. "I... think I misheard you."

"There is a famous painting," June replied, with her hands still clasped together in prayer as she stared out into the night sky, "that claims to show one of the gates of Hell. This painting hangs in St. Jude's, as it happens. I have found myself looking up at it on a number of occasions, but it took me a little while to realize that it shows almost the exact same view that I witnessed tonight when I looked down into the abyss far beneath us."

"Okay," Stella said cautiously, "that's... an unfortunate coincidence, but it doesn't mean anything. It can't. Hell's not a real place."

Sister June turned and glared at her.

"You know what I mean," Stella continued. "It might be a real place, at least for some people, but that doesn't mean anyone believes it's literally underground. That would be a ridiculously literal interpretation."

"Would it?" June asked, raising a skeptical eyebrow. "A gate might lead to a place far away. If that is what we have found here, then it doesn't mean that Hell itself is beneath our feet. It merely means that one of the gates that leads there can be found in this place."

"I consider myself to be quite open-minded," Stella told her, "but even *I* have to draw the line somewhere." She turned to her father, who had made his way over to listen to their conversation as the tent nearby flapped in the growing breeze. "You agree, Dad, right? When religion and history mix, there's only ever going to be one winner. Sure, there are elements of history in religion, but at the end of the day as archaeologists we can't allow ourselves to get distracted by... fairy stories."

Weaver opened his mouth to reply, but for a moment he seemed lost for words until finally he shook his head.

"Of course," he muttered. "Quite right. As tempting as it might be, Sister June, I'm afraid we simply can't consider the idea that what we've found down there is..." His voice trailed off for a few seconds. "It's simply not credible at all. If we voiced such an idea to anyone else, we'd be laughed out of the room and our careers would be over."

"I know what that painting shows," June told him. "Now that I think of it, the similarity is too great to be coincidental. I believe the artist, a Mr. Toyner, experienced some kind of vision that -"

"Wait!" Stella called out, stepping past them both. "Did you see that?"

"What?" Weaver asked.

"I thought..." Her voice trailed off for a moment, but a few seconds later they all heard something bumping against some of the cases stacked near the tent. "One of those damn things has come up here again!"

Grabbing one of the rifles from nearby, she rushed past the cases before stopping to take aim. A strange animal-like squealing sound rang out, and Stella tracked something moving through the darkness before finally she pulled the trigger, and in that moment an even louder cry shook the camp. Lowering the rifle, Stella hesitated before climbing over several boxes and making her way toward the hole that led underground. Weaver, meanwhile, glanced briefly at Sister June before they both hurried over and found Stella standing over the body of some kind of small, vaguely half-human creature on the ground.

"That's one of them," Stella said, sounding a

little breathless now as she looked around to check whether there might be any more intruders. "That's one of the things that attacked me."

"What is it?" Weaver whispered, crouching down to take a closer look. "It's human in shape, but it's the size of a child."

"Be careful," June told him. "Don't get too close."

"It's very thin," Weaver continued, and now the approaching storm was blowing sand through the air as he reached out and touched the creature's shoulder. "It's skin appears to be very pale, and its _"

Suddenly the creature screamed and launched itself at him, knocking him down before scrambling away and throwing itself down the hole, leaving a trail of dark blood across the stones. Stella instinctively took aim and fired again, this time missing the creature as it disappeared from sight; the shot hit some nearby stones harmlessly, and Stella muttered her frustration as she lowered the rifle again.

"What the hell *was* that thing?" Weaver stammered, sitting up and touching the side of his face, where a thick scratch now ran through his cheek. "I've never seen anything like it."

"There are lots of them down there," Stella said, setting the rifle aside. "They're not brave, but I'm not sure they're going to give up, either. Now that we seem to have their attention, I don't exactly know what they want, but we have to find a way to deal with them." She looked down at the blood. "I got that damn thing," she continued. "I shot it right in the head, but somehow it managed to keep going, it's almost as if..."

She hesitated for a few more seconds, before sitting on a nearby rock as tears began to run from her eyes. Leaning forward as Sister June rushed over to comfort her, she started sobbing gently.

"Damn it!" she hissed. "Why am I reacting like this?"

"You're probably in shock," June told her.

"Those things aren't natural," she continued. "When I was down there in the tunnels, they were clawing at me and trying to drag me deeper and deeper, almost as if..."

She turned to June, and for a moment her eyes were filled with a sense of genuine horror.

"As if they were trying to drag me to Hell," she added finally.

"I'm not sure that it's tremendously helpful to think in those terms," June countered.

"But you said it yourself," Stella continued. "You said that's what that place is down there!"

"Yes, but -"

"So what are they? Are they demons?"

"I'm afraid I can't be sure," June told her. "There are lots of conflicting opinions as to what exactly goes on in... that place. They're certainly up to no good, I have to admit that, but my initial belief is that they're not demons, they're more like... assistants."

"Assistants? To demons?"

"Creatures that guard the outer reaches of... that place. If I remember my reading correctly, some believe that they used to be people, that in that place they've become mere servants of demonic masters. They've been reduced to scuttling and crawling about, filled with a kind of childish and mischievous desire to cause trouble. In some cultures, when they've been encountered by the living, they've been referred to as goblins or other entities. Some even believe that they're the origin of the Tenderling myth." She paused for a moment, as if she could scarcely believe what she was saying. "I'm not quite ready to believe that's what we've found, however," she added. "That place down there might look like the painting of Hell, but that doesn't mean that it *is* Hell. The whole thing might just be a coincidence."

"Do you really believe that?" Stella asked.

"It doesn't matter what I believe," June replied. "What matters is that we get out of here and call for help." She turned and looked around. "Where's your father?"

Stella too looked across the camp, and after a moment she got to her feet. Clearly troubled, she hurried around to the far side of the tent, where she saw that one of the boxes had been opened.

"Dad?" she called out, before checking inside the box. "It's gone."

"What's gone?" June asked as she hurried over to join her. "Stella, what's going on? Where's your father?"

Stella hesitated, before rushing over to the hole in the ground and looking down into the darkness below. As sand continued to blow through the air all around, she cupped her hands around her mouth.

"Dad, stop!" she yelled. "Can you hear me? Don't go back down there!"

"Why would he do such a thing?" June asked.

"He's an idiot," Stella said after a moment, turning to her. "He's such an idiot. I can't believe he'd do something so stupid."

"What do you -"

"He's taken the dynamite," she continued, as a sense of fear gripped her voice. "We always carry some in case we need to clear rubble, but he's taken all of it down there. None of this makes sense, Dad would never damage an archaeological site, but I think he's planning to blow that place up. There's only one reason people run off with dynamite, isn't there?"

CHAPTER TWENTY-FOUR

"DAD!" STELLA SHOUTED AS she and June made their way along one of the passageways deep beneath the surface, with only the beams from their flashlights to guide their way. "You have to stop!"

"Wait a moment," June said, struggling to check their route against the map she'd drawn earlier. "I have to be sure that we're going in the right direction. Taking a wrong turn might be disastrous, we could end up trapped down here forever."

"Dad found his way, so we should have no problem."

"We don't *know* that your father found the correct route," June pointed out. "For all we know, he might be lost down here. We can only pray that we're able to find him."

"You can go back up if you're scared."

"I'm not scared," June replied, hurrying to catch up to her once she was sure they were heading in the right direction. "I'm simply worried about the ramifications of what happens here tonight. If I'm right about this being a portal to Hell – and I'm still not certain that I am – then we could cause some serious damage if we mess around. Could we not consider simply sealing the whole place up again and leaving it?"

"That doesn't sound very nun-like to me."

"I'm arguing in favor of restraint," June insisted. "One shouldn't simply go blundering into a situation without considering all the options."

"My father's the one you need to be lecturing," Stella pointed out. "He's the one who's come charging down here with a load of -"

Stopping suddenly, she tilted her flashlight a little and saw Weaver kneeling at the arched gate. He was leaning over packs of dynamite, which he'd set all around the bottom of the gate.

"Dad!" she shouted, hurrying over to him. "Are you out of your mind? You're an archaeologist, you're supposed to be preserving the past, not blowing it up!"

"That was before I realized what was happening here," he stammered, not even looking up at her as he continued to work with the timer. "I had something of a conversion up there when I saw that creature, Stella. I'm not sure what it is, but I saw how much it and its friends hurt you and I simply can't let that happen again." He finally glanced at her. "I'm an archaeologist, that's true, but before that I'm a father. I've got my priorities wrong in the past with Gretchen but I refuse to make that mistake again."

"What are you talking about?" Stella asked.

"Nothing," he said, looking briefly at Sister June again before returning his attention to the timer. "Sister, would you mind escorting my daughter back to the surface? I know what I'm doing down here, but dynamite should always be treated with care and accidents can occasionally happen."

"I'll go back up," Stella said firmly, "but only when you come with me."

"I'll be right behind you," Weaver explained, fumbling a little with the time now as he tried to push the wires into the right slots. "We can't leave this gate open, Stella. If more of those things come through, who knows what might happen to the world?"

Aiming her flashlight ahead, Stella saw movement in the distance She tilted the flashlight a little, and sure enough she saw several more of the goblin-like creatures scurrying back away from the beam.

"They don't like light very much," she

pointed out. "I don't think they like attention, either." Hearing a scuttling sound, she turned to see that one of the creatures was much closer, sneaking toward the dynamite. "Get out of here!" she shouted, aiming the beam directly into its eyes, causing it to scramble away to join the others. "Feeling brave, are you? Come any closer and I'll make you wish you'd never been born! Or died! Whatever!"

The creatures stared back at her, and for a moment she could only watch their haggard faces as she realized that these things had once been human too; reduced to crawling around on the rocky ground, they made for a pathetic sight.

"Are they really dead people?" she asked. "Are you sure about that, Sister June? Are these people who ended up going to Hell and not really fitting in too well?"

"I'm afraid I really don't understand the hierarchies down here," June admitted, "but that would certainly seem to be a reasonable assumption. These poor souls were once like you and I, but I can only suppose that they made terrible choices in their lives if they ended up down here." She watched as one of the creature began to crawl forward, only for it to pull back after a moment. "Now they're doomed to exist like this for all eternity, trapped in endless suffering, barely even able to remember their old lives." She made the sign of the cross against her chest. "I shall pray for them."

"It's ready," Weaver said, struggling a little to get to his feet. "Is everyone happy now? It's going to go off in ten minutes, so that gives us plenty of time to get to the surface and move away from the rocks."

"Away from the rocks?" Stella asked, turning to him. "Is the explosion going to be that big?"

"Almost certainly not," he told her, "but I'd really rather not take any risks. I know there's a sandstorm up there, but we'll have to take our chances." Grabbing Stella by the arm, he began to lead her along the passage. "Sister June, are you coming?" he continued. "I don't know about you, but I certainly don't want to be down here when that thing goes off."

"Of course," June replied, turning to follow them. "I just -"

"Help me!" a gravelly voice called out.

Stopping, June turned to see that one of the creatures had crawled past the dynamite and was now reaching a hand out toward her. She opened her mouth to shout to the others, but for a few seconds she could only stare at the poor wretch as she saw human fear and human sorrow in its eyes.

"Sister," the creature continued, "please... I'm so sorry for what I did in my life. Can't you save me?"

"I..."

Her voice trailed off as the creature crawled a little closer. Further back, a few more of them were starting to scuttle out through the doorway, passing the dynamite as they dared to approach.

"I know what I did was bad," the first creature hissed, "and I know I should have repented while I had the chance, but I'm begging for release. I've been down here for so very long and all I want to do is atone for my sins. Shouldn't I be allowed to have that chance?"

"Sister June, come on!" Stella called out from a little further along the passageway. "Leave them to die!"

"I can't help you," June told the closest creature, as several more inched toward her. "I'm afraid I can't help any of you. Once you're condemned to Hell, there's no way back."

"My name was Walter Foreman," the creature told her. "Sometimes I struggle to remember, and sometimes it's so clear, it feels like it was yesterday. I was a blacksmith and my daughter was causing trouble. Sister, I made such a terrible mistake, but I'm begging for another chance. And if I can't get a chance, then might I at least see my dear Helene one more time? Might I at least tell her that I'm sorry?"

"Help me!" another of the creatures begged,

followed by another and then another as they edged closer and threatened to form a circle around June.

"I can't do anything," June told them, as she touched the simple silver crucifix that hung around her neck. "It's not my place. I can't decide your fates."

"It's not fair!" another of the creatures hissed. "Save me!"

"No, not him!" a third creature snarled, pushing the others back as he lunged forward. "If you're going to save someone, it should be me! Sister, you have to get me out of here! I've suffered enough, I've done my penance and now I deserve the chance to be happy! I promise I won't ever hurt anyone again!"

"Save me instead!" yet another creature begged, grabbing the side of June's leg in an attempt to pull her closer. "I deserve it more than they do! I shouldn't even be down here in the first place, it's all just a big mistake!"

"Stop," June replied, stepping back, "I -"

Before she could finish, she saw that several of the creatures were fiddling with the dynamite. One in particular was messing with the timer, and she watched with a growing sense of horror as it began to turn the dial on the front.

"No!" Weaver shouted, rushing up behind June and grabbing her arm. "The damn thing's changing the countdown! The dynamite's going to

_"

In that instant the packs of dynamite exploded, blasting the entire passageway, sending June and the others crashing back against the wall as the ceiling began to collapse on top of them.

CHAPTER TWENTY-FIVE

AS MORE AND MORE bricks and rocks rained down, June coughed violently and pulled back. She could hear the splitting, groaning sound of another part of the ceiling threatening to fall down, but almost a minute had passed since the explosion and she was starting to hope that the worst effects of the blast were over.

For now.

"Stella!" she called out desperately. "Doctor -"

Before she could finish she broke into another coughing fit. Dust hung in the air as she dropped to her feet; she saw her flashlight nearby and reached out for it, only to find that it was wedged far too firmly beneath some rocks. She tried to pull it out, but the rocks were too heavy and after a few seconds she pulled back. All around she could hear more debris falling own, and in the confusion of the blast she'd lost all sense of her surroundings. Looking around now, she had no idea which way she should go, but she also saw that all of her routes were blocked.

Above, the roof rumbled ominously as if it might be about to collapse.

"Stella!" June shouted as she waved as much dust away from her mouth as possible. "Can you hear me?"

She waited, but she heard no sign of human voices above the jostling of falling bricks.

"Doctor Weaver?" she continued, still hoping against hope that the others might be alright. "If you can hear me, please let me know that you're alright!"

Again she waited.

Again, she heard no reply.

"If you can get to safety," she told them, "you must go. Do you understand? It's far too dangerous down here to try to carry out some kind of rescue mission. If you can hear me and if there's a way out..."

Her voice trailed off as she realized that they would have replied now if they were able. Weaver had been standing right next to her when the dynamite had exploded, but she'd lost track of Stella's position in the passageway. For a moment, as she felt the ground shuddering slightly beneath her feet she couldn't help but wonder just how far down beneath the surface she might be trapped. A few seconds later she felt the ground tilt slightly, and she looked down just in time to see a large crack opening in the rocks. Barely even daring to move a muscle, she realized that the explosion had set off a chain reaction that might not be over yet.

"Alright," she whispered, trying to stay calm, "if -"

Suddenly the ground fell away beneath her. Letting out a startled cry, she tried to grab hold of something – anything – nearby that might keep her safe, but instead she tumbled several feet before falling onto her back and slithering down into a narrow crack. Immediately twisting around, she had to hold her arms up to protect her head as several small rocks rained down against her. The flashlight was still wedged somewhere high up, but its beam was next to useless now as June found herself trapped in almost total darkness down at the bottom of the newly-opened crack in the ground.

Once she'd got her breath back, she realized that her only hope was to try to climb to freedom.

She began to try, only to find that she could barely get a grip on the rocks. After a few seconds the wall to her left began to break apart, and she flinched in case the entire floor fell again. When this failed to happen, she adjusted her position, but she was surprised now to see that a faint flickering light was breaking through a narrow crack running across the floor between her feet.

"What the..."

Crouching down, she leaned closer to the light. For a moment she wondered whether by some miracle she might have been delivered closer to the surface, even if she knew that made no sense at all; the light seemed to have a reddish tinge, and when she place a hand against the ground June realized that the rocks felt slightly warm.

"Dear Lord," she whispered, "pleases give me the strength to get through this. Whatever hurdles you might put in my way, pleases know that I will face them without hesitation. I know that you will guide me to where -"

Before she could finish, the ground beneath her shuddered and dropped down a couple of feet. Letting out a cry, June reached out and steadied herself against the sides, but already she could feel that the ground was unstable and might drop again at any moment.

"I know that you will guide me," she continued, touching the silver crucifix around her neck in the hope that she might find a little more strength. "I know that you will send me to where I am needed and -"

The ground shifted again. June cried out, clinging to the rocky wall as she waited for the movement to subside; she could feel the rocks threatening to break beneath her weight, and more light was starting to get through the cracks near her feet.

"You will send me to where I am needed," she said, struggling to hold back tears, "and I will do my best to complete your work. For thy -"

In that instant the ground gave way completely. June began to fall, only to grab onto one of the rock outcrops at the last moment. With her legs dangling below in thin air, she immediately tried to haul herself up, only to find that she was too weak; she tried again, but for a moment her left hand began to slip slightly and she had to focus in order to maintain her grip. Once she'd managed to stabilize herself, at least for a few seconds, she reached up and tried yet again to pull herself to safety, but she found that any attempt only made her risk falling further.

Feeling heat from below, she hesitated for a

moment before looking down, and finally she saw where the light had been coming from.

Far beneath her dangling feet, a vast opening had been carved out of the ground, revealing a series of concentric rings with small windows drilled into their sides. The rings were arranged in rough layer, and flames were burning in a pit at the bottom. Realizing that something was moving on the rocky sides of the chasm, June blinked in an attempt to clear her vision, and finally she saw thousands of the little goblin-like creatures constantly trying to climb up from the flames, only for them all to slip and fall again; they began to climb again, as if they were trapped forever in a never-ending cycle of escape attempts.

A moment later June realized she could hear a howling sound coming from far below, as if millions of voices were crying out in anguish. She told herself that she had to be wrong, that the sound was simply caused by wind blowing through the vast chasm, yet somehow the voices seemed to twist as they rose ever higher, revealing the begging cries of souls desperate for salvation. As June adjusted her grip and tried to keep from falling, she felt utterly mesmerized by what seemed to be the pit of Hell.

Suddenly her right hand slipped. She tried to

hold on, but her body twisted around until she was hanging from just her left hand; when she tried to reach up, she found that she lacked the strength, and already her left hand was starting to slip. She knew that within seconds she was going to plummet, but her final attempt to reach up with her right hand failed and she could only look down. As her left hand finally fell away, she felt herself starting to drop down into Hell.

Suddenly another hand grabbed her wrist, holding her up. June turned as she felt herself being hauled to safety, and she scrambled to support herself as she was dragged well clear of the pit and thrown onto a stable section of one of the few remaining chambers.

"Stella?" she gasped, dusting herself down as she got to her feet and turned. "Doctor Weaver? I thought you were gone, you really shouldn't have come back to -"

To her shock, she found herself confronted by one of the small goblin-like creatures. Barely able to make the figure out properly in the darkness, June took a step back.

"This way," the figure said, gesturing for her to follow as it began to climb over some rubble. "I'll show you how to get back to the surface."

"Wait!" June called out. "What -"

"Hurry!" the figure shouted back at her. "This part's all going to come down soon, and I don't know whether I'll be able to save you again. You have to get out of here!"

CHAPTER TWENTY-SIX

COUGHING ONCE AGAIN AS she tried to clear her throat, June scrambled to the top of the steps that led to the burial chamber, and then she turned to look back down the way she'd just come.

"Thank you," she said, "but -"

Before she could finish, she saw that the creature was already scampering back down into the darkness.

"Wait!" she called out. "I want to help you! I -"

In that moment part of the ceiling collapsed. Stumbling back, June tripped and fell down, landing hard on the rocky ground just as she saw that the entire roof was falling down and blocking the steps. She crawled forward, but already she could see that the route back down to the underground passages had been firmly blocked.

"Sister June?" Stella gasped, rushing through and grabbing her arm from behind. "I thought you were trapped down there!"

"Yes," June replied, unable to stop staring at the rubble and thinking of the pathetic wretch that had saved her, "I thought I was too." She paused, before turning to look at up at Stella and then seeing that Weaver was standing nearby, resting against the side of the sarcophagus. "Are you both okay?"

"A little bruised," Weaver admitted, wiping some more dirt from the side of his face, "but otherwise I think we shall both live. I must admit, though, that was a little close for comfort. Still, we seem to have sealed off that passage for good, so hopefully no more of those brutish creatures will ever be able to get through."

"I'm not sure they were quite so brutish," June whispered.

"What do you mean?" Stella asked. "What did you see down there, Sister June?"

June looked up at her, but she already knew that she couldn't answer that question. If she even began to admit the truth, that she thought she'd seen a tiny part of Hell, she was likely to be written off as a complete lunatic, and she supposed that there was no need to burden anyone else with the weight of such a revelation. Instead, getting to her feet, she brushed herself down a little more and then took a limping step forward, finding that she was more than a little sore.

"Nothing," she said finally, as she allowed Stella to support her on their slow walk toward the exit. "Nothing at all. I rather think I've had too much excitement, though. I could do with a rest."

"Let's hope that sandstorm has blown over," Weaver muttered.

"Wait," Stella said suddenly, stopping and turning to her father as he continued to lean against the side of the sarcophagus. "What did you mean down there?"

"What are you talking about?" Weaver asked, clearly feeling a little weak.

"You said something about Mum," Stella continued. "Something about priorities. Down here is the only time you've ever really seemed like you were about to open up about her, so what exactly were you talking about?"

"Stella," Weaver replied, "please, I -"

"She died because she waited too long to get medical attention, didn't she?" Stella added. "Don't even bother to deny it, Dad, because I've known the truth for years."

"You have?" he asked.

"I picked up a few whispers here and there," she told him. "I always saw the guilt in your eyes. Eventually I figured it out, but..." She paused, before reaching into her pocket and pulling out a tattered notebook. "This was Mum's diary," she continued. "I found it in her stuff years after she died. She was sick when she wrote the last entries, she knew she had malaria but she also knew how important the project was to you. She was part of the prep work, remember? She did a lot of the research. She was just as invested in the whole thing as you were. In some ways, maybe even more."

"I'm so sorry," Weaver replied, as tears began to fill his eyes. "Stella, I -"

"But she hid the worst of the symptoms," Stella added, before he had a chance to finish. "That's the truth of it. Sure, you might have pushed her to seek help more quickly, but she hid how badly she was suffering because she wanted you to finish your work." She held the notebook up a little higher. "It's all in here, Dad. She knew exactly what she was doing. She knew the risks she was taking."

"But... why?" he asked.

"Because she loved you," Stella replied, "and because the work was just as important to her as well. You realize she was going to insist on having her name added as an author to any papers you wrote about those discoveries, don't you? Please, Dad, this is the 1980s. Men aren't the only ones who are allowed to be a little selfish these days. It's all about equality."

"You knew all this time?" Weaver said, his voice filled with a sense of shock.

"I never quite found the right time to talk to you about it," she admitted. "Plus you were always so closed off, you shut down any time I tried. And maybe, deep down, a tiny part of me wanted you to feel bad." She paused, before stepping forward and holding the notebook out to him. "I guess arrogance runs in the family just a little," she said with a faint smile. "I'm sorry, Dad. You, me and Mum... none of us were perfect. There's a lot more in her last diary, though. You should read it. Do you have any idea how much she loved you?"

"I don't deserve to read this," he stammered.

"You've lived in your own private hell for long enough," She told him. "It's time to heal."

"Thank you," he replied, taking the notebook and holding it as if he couldn't quite believe that it was real. "Thank you so much, Stella. I finally feel as if I can look you in the eye again." He stared at the notebook for a few more seconds, holding it in his trembling hands, before turning to his daughter again. "I never wanted to keep the truth from you," he added, as a faint gasping sound began to rise from the sarcophagus behind him. "I always felt such guilt, Stella, as if I'd robbed you of your mother. I still feel that way a little."

"You don't need to," Stella told him. "We're a family of selfish bastards. But for what it's worth, and just in case you need to hear it, I forgive -"

Suddenly a rotten figure lunged up from the

sarcophagus and grabbed Weaver from behind, pulling him back and clawing at his throat. Stella immediately rushed forward, but June held her back and they watched in horror as the corpse tore Weaver's head clean off his shoulders. Throwing the head aside, the corpse began to drink frantically from the blood that was gushing from the dead man's severed neck, before turning to June and Stella and letting out an angry scream.

"Dad!" Stella gasped.

"I was worried that something like this might happen," June replied, as the figure shoved Weaver's body to the ground and took a stumbling step forward, "but in all the emotion of the moment it slipped from my mind."

"What *is* that thing?" Stella asked.

"I don't think we should stick around to find out," June said, grabbing her by the hand and pulling her out of the chamber, leading her toward the ladder. "We must get out of here as fast as we can. I'm afraid there's no time to look back."

Reaching the ladder, she began to push Stella up.

"Climb!" she hissed. "Get to the top before it's too late!"

The rotten corpse was already stumbling after them, making its way slowly but surely from the chamber. June waited until Stella was far enough up the ladder, and then she too began to climb, managing to evade the corpse's grasping hand by a matter of inches.

"I don't think this ladder's going to hold both of us!" Stella called out, and sure enough the ladder's sides were starting to break free from the rungs. "It was never designed to support the weight of two people!"

"Hurry!" June yelled, as she looked down and saw to her horror that the figure was starting to climb after them "It's not just two people now! It's three!"

"It's not going to stay up!" Stella shouted, reaching out to steady herself against the rocky wall for a moment. "Sister June, it's going to break!"

"Just climb as fast as you can!" June called back to her as she felt the rotten hand once more trying to grab her heel from below. "Stella, hurry! There's no time to waste! We have to get out of here!"

CHAPTER TWENTY-SEVEN

AS SOON AS SHE reached the surface, June threw herself over the edge, only to let out a gasp as she felt sand blasting against her face. For a moment she was entirely disorientated; she lay on the ground, gasping for breath but succeeding only in getting more and more sand into her mouth. When she tried to sit up, she felt strong wind blowing against her side, and already her face hurt as the sandstorm raged.

"Sister June!"

With her eyes clamped shut for protection, June felt a hand grabbing her from nearby. Stumbling to her feet, she allowed herself to be led through the storm until finally the sand stopped hitting her; daring to open her eyes, she was almost blinded by the beam of a flashlight, which was then lowered to reveal Stella's horrified face staring back at her as the two women stood in the tent.

Looking around, June saw that the tent's fabric walls were fluttering fast and hard as the storm persisted. A howling sound was filling the night air, and a moment later several of Doctor Weaver's boxes blew past with their contents flying out and scattering across the rocks.

"So this is a sandstorm, is it?" June said breathlessly, looking down at her hands and seeing that they'd already been scratched by the sand swirling through the air. "Well, I'm starting to see why they can be do destructive. One should never fail to respect the sheer fury of nature."

"What *was* that thing?" Stella asked, staring out into the storm.

"I think it -"

June hesitated, before turning and watching as the flashlight's beam cut through the flying sand. For a moment she half-expected to see a figure stumbling forward, emerging from the darkness of the storm.

"It killed my father," Stella continued, her voice trembling with shock. "That thing, I mean. It just came up out of the sarcophagus and it..."

Her voice trailed off.

"I'm not entirely sure what it was," June said after a moment, as she remembered the rotten hand touching her heel from below as she'd climbed up the ladder. "For some reason, the body in the sarcophagus suddenly became animated. Clearly your father had no idea that such a thing was about to happen, or -"

Before she could finish, they both heard an angry, furious scream ringing out through the storm.

"Did it follow us?" Stella asked, taking a step back further into the tent. "Sister June, please tell me that thing doesn't know how to climb ladders."

"Well, I suppose ladders have been around for a while," June replied, as she too stepped back. "It might well have... known what a ladder is, at least. When it was alive."

"Was it some kind of zombie?"

"I'm sure zombies aren't real," June told her. "They can't be. I mean, vampires maybe, and mermaids and..."

Her voice trailed off, and for a few seconds she realized that the idea of a zombie actually wasn't so utterly strange given her recent history.

"Well, I'm sure it's not a zombie," she added finally. "It can't be. It just... isn't..."

"Then what else would you call it?"

"I'm afraid I really don't know," June replied, "but that's neither here nor there now, not if -"

Suddenly something bumped against the outside of the tent, hitting the fabric next to June.

Shocked, she turned and pulled back, but hands were clawing now at the fabric as if the figure out there was trying to make its way inside.

"That's him!" Stella hissed. "Or her! Whatever the hell that thing was down there, it's up here now!"

"It would seem to be," June muttered, before slipping the silver crucifix from around her neck.

"Do you seriously think *that's* going to help?" Stella asked.

"Well, I would certainly hope so," June replied, holding the crucifix in her shaking hands. "I'm afraid it's really my only idea right now." She watched as the clawing hands moved further across the fabric, making their way slowly but surely toward the opening. "The warnings on the tomb down there seemed to be addressed not to those of us coming from above, but to those approaching the tomb from below," she continued. "Tell me, how much did you actually manage to translate?"

"Very little," Stella said as they both watched the hands still scratching at the tent. "There was the usual stuff about not daring to enter the tomb, about staying out or facing some terrible fate." She adjusted her grip on the flashlight. "There was some pretty dramatic stuff, too, about trapping someone in Hell."

"Trapping him in Hell," June whispered,

before turning to Stella. "That's it! Whoever this was, he was consigned to Hell!"

"How does that help us?"

"It doesn't," June explained, "but at least it makes sense. When your father detonated that dynamite, he sealed the gateway to Hell, so the tomb was released and became part of the mortal world again. Whatever hold was placed on it, whatever power was being used to keep the dead fellow in his tomb, it must have ended once the tomb was no longer connected to Hell."

"Are you even listening to the words coming out of your mouth right now?" Stella asked.

"Now he's free again," June continued.

"Which means he's up and about?" Stella said, her voice filled with an increasing sense of dead. "Well, isn't that just the best news we've had tonight?"

"Whoever he was," June continued, "somebody went to great lengths many years ago to bury him down there. They must have been extremely keen to make sure that he was unlikely to rise from the grave. In fact, I'm starting to think that we were very foolish to even consider tampering with what was down there."

"And now we've screwed their plan up royally," Stella pointed out, before furrowing her brow. "Hey, I don't see the hands anymore. I don't think he's still out there." She took another step back. "Do you think that means he's given up? It's not like he actually still had eyes, and his ears must have been pretty rotten too, so what if he just doesn't realize where we are?"

"That would be extremely convenient," June suggested, "although experience tells me that such things rarely happen quite so neatly. These things have a habit of coming back when one least expects them."

They stood in silence for a moment, listening to the storm swirling outside as the tent creaked and groaned under the onslaught. Every few seconds a particularly loud bumping sound would catch their attention in one corner or another, but so far the tent seemed to be holding up reasonably well and there was no further sound of the rotten figure that had emerged from the tomb.

Even June, who had been sure they couldn't escape so easily, caught herself wondering whether by some miracle the rotten man might simply have faded away into the night.

"This storm could last for hours," Stella said finally. "I've never been in one, at least not a proper one like this, but Dad told me about them and apparently they're pretty much your worst nightmare. It's like walking through sandpaper or -"

She stopped suddenly, furrowing her brow.

"Dad," she added, and now her voice was tinged with sadness. "He's really gone. All those times I hated him so much, and now -"

Suddenly the fabric tore open behind her. Letting out a shocked cry, Stella turned just as the rotten figure lunged through, grabbing her by the shoulders and quickly forcing herself down onto the ground. Stella tried to push him away, but the dead man placed a rotten hand around her throat and began to squeeze. Letting out an agonized scream of anger, the figure leaned down toward her as if it meant to bite into the side of her neck.

"Leave her alone!" June shouted, rushing forward and holding out the silver crucifix.

The rotten figure turned to her and snarled, revealed thick strands of flesh still somehow clinging to what remained of its bones. There were no eyes in its sockets, just empty gaps with a few scraps of torn skin on the sides.

"Sister June, help!" Stella gasped.

"Leave her alone!" June yelled again, stepping closer. "The power of the Lord commands you to let her go!"

Pushing the crucifix into the creature's face, June forced him away from Stella. Tilting his head back, the figure looked up into the stormy night sky as he was forced partially back out of the tent. June had the crucifix pressed against his features, but the raging sandstorm was already blasting the rotten meat away from his features and after a moment his body began to decompose and fall apart entirely.

June screamed as she pushed harder than ever, and finally the rotten figure from the sarcophagus fell back as the storm ripped his already-flimsy body to pieces. After a few more seconds, his bones began to blow away.

June pulled back, landing hard on the floor of the tent as more sand blew through the opening.

CHAPTER TWENTY-EIGHT

ZURICH WAS BUSY THAT night, with late-night party-goers hurrying from one venue to another and some stopping to rest in the doorways of shuttered shops. A few cafes were still open, catering to anyone who wanted.

"Your coffee," the waiter said, setting a cup down on one of the tables. "I hope you enjoy."

"Thank you," John replied, before spotting a familiar figure taking a seat nearby. He watched for a moment, until Eloise noticed him. "Hi there," he continued. "I'm sorry, I think we met a little earlier during the night."

"I don't know what -"

Seemingly somewhat dazed, she stared at him for a moment before nodding.

"Oh, right," she said after a few more

seconds. She seemed awkward now, barely able to think of anything to say, before spotting the book on the table. "Good read?"

"It's a little dry," John admitted, holding the book up. "Ignore the dark stain on the cover. That's just... coffee. It's totally not in the shape of a hand-print."

Leaning closer, Eloise peered at the title.

"I don't even know what language that is," she told him.

"It's very old," he explained, turning the book around so that he could see it himself. "Older than you might think possible. This is a copy of an ancient text that many people wouldn't even believe could exist. As far as I'm aware, it's the only text that survived from a very old civilization. It's so unusual that most scholars dismissed it long ago." He paused, staring at the book, before starting to flick through it. "Parts of it make sense, though."

"You can read it?"

"It's sort of a gift," he suggested. "Besides, I've been studying this stuff for a while. It's about an ancient civilization, supposedly the first ever, that grew up around twelve..."

His voice trailed off for a moment.

"Do you want to hear this?" he asked.

"Sure," she replied, forcing a smile. "Sorry, it's been a long night. To be honest, I feel a little cold."

"So they grew up around these twelve vents in the ground," he continued, taking his book and coffee and moving over to sit at her table. "Each of these vents ran extremely deep below, some of the ancient kings believed they were the twelve gates that led to Hell. Anyway, eventually these civilizations developed around the vents, guarding them, but after a while they began to move away. Got to head to where there grass is greener, right? And over the years, I suppose later generations forgot their sacred purpose."

"Right," Eloise said cautiously, as if she wasn't quite sure whether or not he'd lost his mind.

"So they each took their biggest and baddest, most evil citizens, and ritually slaughtered them. Because you can't just leave one of these gates unattended, right?"

"Right," she said again. "I mean... sure..."

"And they placed them in these tombs that they sealed over the gates," he told her, "and they inscribed them with all these warnings, with the plan being that these tombs would sort of... mark the boundary between Hell below and the world of man above. After that, the civilizations moved on and headed to different parts of the world. Europe, Asia, all the usual spots that feature in the history books. Over time they all forgot where they came from, but if you believe what's in this book, the original vents were left sealed out there somewhere, hidden underground far from prying eyes."

"Okay," Eloise said after a few seconds. "I mean, that sounds like a... cool story, I suppose."

"It's said that if anyone could find one of those vents, they'd be able to make their way down to Hell," John continued. "Can you imagine that? They'd have to break through the tomb first, and that wouldn't be easy. I mean, I'm sure part of the tale have been twisted over the years thanks to a kind of... Chinese whispers. It still makes you wonder whether there might be anything to it, though."

"Does it?"

"Doesn't it?"

"It sounds a little hokey," she suggested. "If any of that stuff had any basis in truth, don't you think more people would know about it?"

"They might," John admitted. "But they might keep quiet about it all."

"It wouldn't just be in that one book, would it?"

"You raise a good point," he said with a sigh. "Hey, how are you doing tonight, anyway? When I bumped into you a few hours ago, I picked up this real sense of sadness. Don't take this the wrong way, but I have a kind of sixth sense when it comes to these things. I actually would have followed you and tried to make things alright, if it wasn't for the fact that I was kind of in a rush to get to a certain bookshop before it closed."

"You must have really wanted to read that book."

"I did," he muttered, "but I've got what I wanted from it now. I know plenty about those vents, and about what they were there for, and about the civilization that controlled them. They were a strange lot. They lived all those thousands of years ago, and they called themselves the First Order. Funny name, huh?" He paused, before setting it down on the cobbles and taking a lighter from his pocket. After a few seconds, he managed to get the book burning. "Done. You know, book-burning really went out of fashion a while back. I understand the reasons, but sometimes I wonder whether it might occasionally be a good idea."

"Why are you doing that?" Eloise asked.

"Because I've read it and I don't need to read it again," he told her, "and because it's not the kind of book that should be left just sitting around for anyone to find."

"And you read it all tonight?"

"The parts I needed," he replied, before downing his coffee and getting to his feet. "Then again," he added, "I suppose I should have at least made some notes, just in case I forget some details when they're not fresh in my mind." He watched as the book turned to ash, and then he put a hand on Eloise's shoulder. "I suppose it's too late now. I could jot something down, but then I find it's often so hard to sum everything up in writing. I wish I had some other way of recording..."

Pausing, he stared down at his hand, which rested on her shoulder for a moment longer before he pulled it back.

"I'm so sorry," he whispered. "I thought..."

His voice trailed off, and then he looked at Eloise's right ear. After a moment, he leaned down and moved his lips closer, before whispering something.

"Sorry about that," he continued, finally taking a step back. "You've obviously had a heavy night. I suspect you were tempted to do something bad, but the sun'll be up soon and I think you should reconsider and try to move on with things instead. As best you can, at least. It's never too late to try for a second chance. I need you to forget that you saw me tonight but remember what I just told you. Do you think you can manage that, Eloise?"

"Huh?" She looked up at him as if she'd never set eyes on him before in her life. "I'm sorry, do I know you?"

"No, you do not," he said with a smile as he turned and walked away. "Good girl, Eloise. I'll see you again, one day, and I'm very sorry for what's going to have to happen. I might be able to avoid it, but most likely not. Until then... well, you know what you've got to do."

Looking around, Eloise felt completely discombobulated. She saw a waiter clearing some nearby tables and considered asking for something, but at the last moment she reasoned that there was no real point. Instead she got to her feet and, despite feeling a little unsteady, she turned and made her way across the square. All she knew in that moment was that she had to make everything right again.

***

The edges of the torn tent moved gently as a light breeze blew through the bright morning air. The sun was already rising, and the storm had passed a few hours earlier. Already the morning was starting to get hotter.

"Stupid ankle," Stella muttered, sitting on one of the beds in the tent as she examined the makeshift bandage that Sister June had put in place for her. "At least I could have had a cool injury, but no, it's my dumb ankle."

"It's badly sprained," June replied, standing at the torn opening before reaching down and picking her crucifix out from the remains of the rotten corpse. "In my experience, a sprain can often be as bad as a break. Worse, even. At least a clean break will often heal fairly quickly, whereas a sprain can involve all sorts of -"

Before she could finish, she realized she

could hear the sound of a distant motor. Looking up, she spotted one of the planes high in the sky. She blinked, scarcely able to believe her luck, but sure enough the plane continued on its way.

"Grab the flare gun!" Stella said, before trying to get up and immediately letting out a gasp of pain as she slumped back down. "Hurry! I don't want to sit around here for a moment longer than I have to!"

Rushing across the tent, June grabbed the flare gun and headed outside.

"Do you remember how it works?" Stella called after her. "Do you remember what I told you?"

"I remember!" June said, hurrying past the rocks and then stopping as she saw the plane in the distance. Although it looked too far away, she supposed that she had to at least try, so she raised the gun and fired.

A flare blasted up into the sky, burning bright red against the vast blue.

"Did it work?" Stella yelled. "Sister June, did it work? You didn't do something stupid like fire it into the ground, did you?"

"No, I didn't do that," June replied through gritted teeth, and in that moment she felt her heart lift as she saw the plane turning and starting to make its way closer. "I think they saw us!" she shouted. "We're going to be rescued!"

***

"It's good to be home," Elizabeth Tate said as she and her husband carried their suitcases away from the taxi and down the steps toward their front door. "I know we're back a little earlier than we planned, but -"

Stopping suddenly, she saw a figure sitting on the ground just a little way ahead.

"Eloise?" her husband Henrik said cautiously. "Sweetheart, are you okay?"

"Huh?" Eloise replied, opening her eyes and looking up at them, them stumbling to her feet. "Oh, right. Sure. You're home a bit early."

"What happened?" Elizabeth said, stepping toward her daughter and putting a hand on the side of her face. "Sweetheart, I hope you don't mind me saying this, but you look absolutely dreadful."

"Long night," Eloise said, forcing a meager smile that fooled no-one. "Busy night, at least. I think so, anyway. I can't actually remember too much of it, but I've got a splitting headache. Sorry, guys, I know I'm probably the last person you want to find sitting on your doorstep like this, but I suppose..."

Her voice trailed off as she realized that she wasn't entirely sure how she'd reached the doorstep in the first place. She supposed she must have made her way through the city, yet somehow that entire memory seemed to be missing from her mind.

"I must have walked," she said uncertainly, "or... I suppose I might have got a taxi."

"Let's head inside," Henrik said, stepping past her and unlocking the front door, then carrying his suitcase inside. "It's always weird to smell your own place when you get back, isn't it? You start to wonder if that's how your home always smells. Not that it's bad, it just seems a little... fusty."

"Sure does," Eloise replied, slipping past him and grabbing the envelope she'd left previously, then sliding it into her pocket before anyone could notice. "You guys must be exhausted, though, so actually I think I might leave you to unpack and I can pop back later. How does that sound?"

"Darling, it's up to you," Elizabeth said, clearly a little confused by her daughter's behavior. "If you're hungry, I'm sure I can rustle up something from the freezer, perhaps a -"

"I'll call," Eloise continued, already rushing out the door and heading to the steps, walking so fast that she almost tripped. "Or maybe tomorrow, I'm not sure. I arranged for the day off work today so I might just try to sleep this headache off. Sorry to be weird, I'll be in touch!"

Once she reached the road, she began to make her way toward the nearest bus stop. Her mind was racing and she really couldn't remember much of the previous night. Reaching the stop she pulled the envelope from her pocket and took out the note that she'd written, but to her surprise she found that the letters no longer made sense, as if they were written in some other language that she didn't understand and that seemed only vaguely familiar.

CHAPTER TWENTY-NINE

FOOTSTEPS RANG OUT IN the distance as another nurse made her way across the ward.

"This isn't how Dad would have wanted things to end," Stella said, sitting in her hospital bed and staring down at what remained of her tattered notebook. "All that work, all those risks, and what do we have to show for it? Nothing."

"I'm sure that's not quite accurate," June told her. "You discovered a great deal."

"Yes, but we don't have any proof," Stella pointed out, "and without proof, I'd be a laughing stock if I started rambling on about hidden passages and gates and ancient languages." She paused for a moment. "And that'd be before I ever got a chance to mention weird little goblin-like monsters and entrances to Hell and some kind of zombie."

She swallowed hard, and clearly she was still trying to get her head around everything that had happened.

"Two men came to visit me this morning," she continued. "They made it very clear that the site out there is now government property. Not that I thought there really was much of a government out there in that part of the Sahara, but I'm pretty sure they were covering for whoever really sent them. They asked me if I'd saved anything from the site, and when I admitted that I hadn't, they told me that I really shouldn't ever try to go back there. They also said that they'd arrange for the sponsorship of any other project I want to set up anywhere else, so I suppose I shouldn't complain too much. There's still lots to be done out there in the big wide world."

"You don't seem too excited."

"We were so close to uncovering something sensational," she pointed out, "but my visitors earlier let me know in no uncertain terms that I wouldn't find it if I went back. At best I'd be wasting my time, and at worst I'd be risking walking into an unfortunate... accident. They said they'd recovered Dad's body, though, and that it's already on its way to England. I can arrange a funeral when I'm back."

"I see," June muttered. "I fear their early involvement might be partly my fault. I telephoned the First Order this morning and let them know my findings. I'm so sorry, Stella. They move very quickly."

"It's not your fault," Stella replied. "I'm not some emotionally incontinent fool who goes around fighting battles I can't win. I know when to take a step back." She paused again. "I just wish I'd been able to save Dad. I hope when he died, he didn't think that I hated him."

"I don't think that's possible," June replied, stepping forward and placing a hand on the younger woman's shoulder. "He was so very proud of you. I barely knew him at all, but that pride shone through so very clearly. He'd want you to continue your work."

"Sister June?" one of the nurses said, stepping into the doorway. "The taxi's here to take you to the airport."

"Thank you," June told her, before reaching into her pocket and taking out a small object wrapped in a napkin. "Stella, there's this one thing I'd like you to have."

Reaching out, Stella took the napkin and opened it to reveal a fragment of stone with several strange letters on its surface.

"Is this -"

"From the chamber, yes," June said with a faint smile. "It must have got caught in my things on the way up, I'm not entirely sure how I ended up with it, but I just thought you might like to keep it as a kind of reminder of what you discovered down there. Even if you don't do anything with it on a professional level, you can always remember that you and your father discovered something truly astonishing."

"Thank you," Stella replied, looking up to hear with a tearful expression. "I suppose it's nice to know there are still mysteries out there in the world, waiting to be found. Dad and I might have screwed up this one, but I'll consider that to have been a practice run. *Next* time I uncover a previously unknown ancient civilization that might change our entire understanding of human history, I'm going to be much better prepared."

***

Sitting on a seat at the airport, waiting for her flight to be called, June stared at a large poster on the opposite wall. The poster showed several camels making their way through the desert, and she couldn't help but reflect that just a few days earlier she herself had been riding one of those magnificent creatures.

"I certainly get around," she whispered to herself.

Spotting movement beyond one of the windows, she got to her feet and walked across the waiting area. Reaching the window, she looked out and saw that a large unmarked plane had stopped near the runway, and that several black vehicles were now parked close to the steps that had been wheeled into position. The door at the front of the plane was already open, and a moment later several men in dark suits made their way down onto the tarmac, where they were greeted by other men in dark suits mixed with what appeared to be a number of soldiers. The whole scene radiated a sense of pumped-up self-importance.

A shudder passed through June's chest as she realized that these individuals might well be connected to the events out in the desert. In fact, she was unable to think of an alternative explanation.

For the next few minutes, she watched as the men in suits talked on the tarmac. One or two of them occasionally touched something in their ears, before finally they stepped aside and two more people emerged from the plane. One of these people was a man holding a parasol, providing shade for the sun as the other person – seemingly a frail woman – began to make her way down the steps. June watched the woman's painfully slow progress, but any sorrow she might have felt for the woman quickly made way for an entirely different and unexpected feeling, to which she was by no means accustomed.

A shudder passed through her body as she realized that she knew this woman.

She had no idea how, or where from, but in that moment June felt certain that she'd met the woman before. She couldn't even begin to imagine who it might be, yet she felt as if some kind of pure evil was radiating from the woman's body and reaching out to her from across the tarmac. Unable to avert her gaze, June watched as the woman was escorted to a waiting limousine and helped inside. At the last moment the parasol was taken down and June caught the briefest glimpse of the woman's face, but the limousine's door soon swung shut and June was left feeling as if she'd been on the verge of recognizing the new arrival.

"Sister June?"

Startled, she turned to see a young man standing next to her.

"I'm sorry," he said, "I didn't mean to disturb you."

"No, it's fine," she replied. "Is it time to board the plane?"

"I think so, in a minute," he told her. "I was asked to come and relay a message to you. Someone phoned the security office and asked me to come and find you. That's never actually happened before, I didn't even know it was possible, but... I got the impression that it was very important."

"Evidently," June said. "Can I be of any assistance?"

"I just have to tell you that there's been a

change of plans," he explained. "The person on the phone said you'd understand. A car will be waiting for you at Heathrow, and apparently it won't be taking you directly back to the convent. Does that make sense?"

"To a certain degree," June said cautiously, "but if the car won't be taking me to the convent, then where *will* it be taking me?"

"They didn't get to that part," the man replied. "Sorry."

"Are you sure this message is meant for me?" she asked. "I'm sorry, it's just that usually there are years and years between my assignments, and I was rather hoping for a nice long rest after all this business."

"I'm just the messenger," he said, clearly feeling a little awkward, before turning to look at the gate as a voice boomed out over the speakers. "That's your flight being called right now," he added, before picking up her suitcase. "Come on, let me carry this for you."

"There's really no need."

"It's no trouble at all," he told her with a smile. "Please, follow me."

June turned to go with him, but at the last second she glanced out the window again, just in time to see the limousine driving away. Now that the strange arrival was out of sight, she felt a little less troubled and she told herself that she must have been wrong. The individual under the parasol had probably just been some local dignitary, and there was really no need to start inventing suspicions where there were none. She knew she'd been through something of an ordeal, and she supposed that she was simply a little more jumpy than usual.

After a moment she turned and began making her way toward the gate, where the nice young man was waiting with her suitcase. As she walked, she couldn't help wondering why the First Order apparently wanted her to undertake another assignment so quickly, and where they could possibly want her to go next.

CHAPTER THIRTY

"CLEAR A PATH!" A voice called out, as several flashlights cast their beams through the darkness. "Clear the way! Somebody clear the way for our guest!"

"It's just a little further," Cardinal Abruzzo explained as he held the old woman's hand, helping her pick a path through the rubble. "We're very nearly there."

"I'm not an invalid," Sister Josephine replied from beneath her black veil, although she sounded distinctly out of breath as she stepped around some rocks on the ground. "I managed to get down that ladder, did I not? If I can do that, I think I should be okay walking in a more-or-less straight line."

"Of course, but -"

"If I'd known you were going to fuss so

much," she continued, "I would have left you in Rome and brought Cardinal Boone instead. Even if that would have meant putting up with his flatulence and bad breath."

"I'm sorry," Abruzzo replied as they reached the end of the passage and stopped. "So this is the gate, or at least what's left of it. We have some men digging through the ruins as we speak. Obviously we need to work out what is and what isn't part of the gate, but I'm confident that we've managed to outline a clear process that'll give us results before too long. And of course we're erring on the side of caution; when in doubt, we ship it all out just to be sure."

"Every scrap of brick and stone must be located," she replied, before slowly pulling the veil aside to reveal her heavily-scarred face. She noticed that some of the workers reacted to her appearance with shock, but she very deliberately avoided look at them or even acknowledging their presence. "To think that after all this time, we've finally found one of the twelve ancient gates that our ancestors guarded so dearly."

"Are you sure?"

She turned to him.

"I just figured," he continued, "that if people from the First Order have been searching for one of these gates for so long, we should be careful to make sure that we've really found one. Wouldn't it be kind of easy to come up with a false positive?"

"I read Sister June's report myself," Josephine told him. "Every word, over and over again. Believe me, there's enough detail in there for me to be certain. For all her faults, June isn't exactly given to hyperbole. Based on her comments alone, I'm certain that this is what we're after."

"It's a shame it's in pieces," Abruzzo pointed out.

"That slows us down," she admitted, "but it does not stop us. "The gate can be taken from this place and put back together. In some ways, this brief interruption actually benefits us, since it takes away the need to make certain key decisions. The gate will be taken to Rome and restored, and then -"

"Are you sure that's wise?"

Josephine turned to him.

"It's one thing to have this gate down here under the ground," he continued unable to hide a sense of fear, "but is it really a good idea to have it out in the open in Rome?"

"It won't be out in the open," she told him. "It will be at the First Order's most heavily-guarded facility, where it can be looked after and contained properly. We have people who have trained their whole lives for this moment. The two of us should not try to get in their way. They must be allowed to continue their work without delay."

"Of course," Abruzzo replied, "I would

never think to disagree with you."

"Our people have been searching for the gates for so long now," she continued, turning to look at the rubble again. "The fact that we ever lost them at all is a crime, but at least we have been able to put part of that right. We don't need all twelve of the gates, we only need one, and now it's in our possession. Once it has been rebuilt, the First Order can finally fulfill its true destiny. A destiny that was cruelly snatched away from us so many years ago."

"And what about Sister June?"

"Ah, yes," Josephine said as a smile spread across her lips, reaching up to the thick scar on her left cheek. "She has done well, has she not?"

"She certainly has," Abruzzo admitted, "but I imagine her work is over now." He paused for a moment. "Should I give the order to have her killed? She should be on a plane back to England at the moment, it would be easy to have that plane experience a minor malfunction. We'd barely even have to get our hands dirty."

"And let her die so quickly and painlessly?" Josephine replied. "I think not. After everything that little bitch put me through in Switzerland twenty-five years ago, I believe I have the right to make her suffer first."

"But -"

"Don't let this concern you," Josephine added. "I've already made the arrangements. Sister

June is to be picked up at Heathrow and driven directly to her final assignment. She's going back to where all of this started for her, to the one place that she barely survived when she was younger."

"You mean -"

"Holdham Hall," Josephine continued, her voice almost purring with anticipation. "She so very nearly died there as a child. This time, there will be no escape. She *should* have died there, so really, I'm merely making sure that her destiny is respected." She watched the bricks for a moment longer. "Believe me," she added finally, "I know exactly what I'm doing. There is simply no way that Sister June can possibly survive a second nightmare at that place. She has served us so very well. Now the time has come for her to die."

***

"Damn it!" Eloise hissed, leaning against the sink in her kitchen. "Pull your head together or you're going to end up losing your whole goddamn mind!"

Having been home for several hours now, and having tried but failed to take a nap, Eloise felt now as if her thoughts were rushing too fast for her to ever sleep again. She barely even remembered the events of the previous night, although she knew she'd wandered the streets of Zurich for hours and hours before meeting that strange man again.

Something about him had seemed very off-putting, as if she'd sensed there was something not quite right about the entire situation, and she'd tried replaying the encounter over and over again in her mind.

He'd whispered something into her ear as he was leaving, something that had sent a shiver through her body, yet now she couldn't remember the words. Sometimes, for a few seconds at a time, she wasn't even able to remember the man at all. Instead the encounter seemed to flit in and out of her memories almost randomly.

"What was it?" she asked out loud.

Again she heard the man's voice, yet somehow she couldn't quite break through the sound and make sense of any of the words.

"Okay," she said finally, glancing at her own reflection in the door of the microwave and immediately seeing the fear in her eyes. "Here's what you're going to do. You're going to stop being such an idiot, and you're going to get on with your life. You've still got so much to live for, so much to do, and there's no point dwelling on..."

Her voice trailed off. After a moment, feeling as if someone might be standing behind her, she turned and looked across the kitchen.

Nothing.

"Hello?" she called out, still worried. "Is anyone here?"

She waited.

Silence, but the room seemed strangely cold.

"If there's anyone here," she continued, "then you should know that I'm armed." Realizing that this was an obvious lie, she looked around for anything she might be able to use as a weapon; when that failed, she decided to simply try to bluff her way through the situation. "I know martial arts," she continued, once again resorting to a lie. "I can defend myself!"

Another lie.

"Or you're just a ghost," she said, realizing that there was still no sign of anyone. "No, that's crazy. There's no such thing as ghosts, so there can't be one here. You're nothing but... random sounds."

Still, she waited for a few more seconds, just to be certain.

"And now you're yelling at shadows," she muttered, leaning her head back for a moment. "Great. Come on, Eloise, you're better than this. You've got work tomorrow, if you can manage to make your way to the bus stop. You just need to rest today and get rid of this stupid headache."

She took a deep breath, but she could still feel a dull ache in the back of her skull. Looking across the kitchen again, she told herself that sleep would make everything better, but after a few seconds her lips parted and she whispered one very unfamiliar word.

"Shadborne."

She swallowed hard, but now she felt the urge to say the word again.

"Shadborne."

She listened, almost expecting to hear someone reply.

"Shadborne," she said for a third time.

Furrowing her brow, she wondered why that word – a name, perhaps? - had left her mouth. She felt fairly certain that she'd never heard it before in her life, and now as she leaned back and gripped the counter she worried that somehow another mind was ripping its way to the surface of her thoughts. She told herself again and again that she was imagining things, and that she was just letting the events of the past few days get to her, but finally she slid down until she was sitting on the floor, and she put her hands on the sides of her head as she squeezed her eyes tight shut and tried to drown out the rushing sense of another presence.

"Stop!" she gasped, as she heard the sound of drums beating somewhere in the distance, accompanied by hundreds of voices chanting rhythmically together. The voices were becoming so loud and so confused, they seemed almost to be combining to form the sound of rushing water. "Go away! Why won't you just leave me alone? Why -"

Stopping suddenly, she found herself staring

straight ahead as the drumming sound came to an abrupt halt. She hesitated, gripped by a growing sense of fear, and then slowly she reached up and touched the side of her neck. As she searched for a pulse, she realized now that more than anything she was desperate for the drums to return.

"Please," she whimpered as tears began to roll down her cheeks. "Come back."

She searched for a few more seconds, and then she tried her wrists, but still she could find no pulse; in fact, she could find no sign of life at all, and when she touched the side of her own neck again she realized that she was so desperately cold. In that moment, as she finally understood why her heard wasn't beating, she screamed.

***

Several miles away, police cars stood parked by the side of a river near Zurich. Police officers stood around and watched as divers began to haul a woman's dead body out of the water.

EPILOGUE

BRIGHT AFTERNOON SUNLIGHT CAUGHT the mushroom's yellow surface. A moment later a pair of lips moved closer and blew away a few last remaining chunks of dirt.

"And there we have it," Fred said, turning the mushroom around to admire it properly. "You know, Stu, you can buy chanterelles from dealers, but they never taste as good. Some mushrooms you just have to pick yourself and cook quickly, so they still taste fresh."

"How good can one mushroom be?" Stu asked, his voice dripping with skepticism. "I mean, how can it make it worthwhile traipsing out here? If you ask me, mushrooms are just stupid slightly spongy things that shouldn't get anywhere near a kitchen."

"You're not exactly a sophisticated fellow, are you?"

"I know what I like, and mushrooms aren't it. Maybe with a full English breakfast, but even then they're usually the worst past. I'm sorry, Fred, but you'll never get me excited about the damn things."

"Wait until I fry a few of these up with butter and serve them with scrambled eggs," Fred replied, dropping the mushroom into his pot before crouching down to pick some more. "Just promise me one thing, okay? Keep your mouth shut and don't tell anyone where we found these. I'd hate for some other bastard to come and pick them all."

"They're only mushrooms," Stu muttered, leaning against a nearby tree. "You're acting like they're as valuable as truffles. If you ask me, this whole situation is completely insane. Give me a steak or some bacon any day, not some stupid yellow mushrooms."

"You'll learn eventually," Fred replied, putting the last of the picked mushrooms into his pot before getting to his feet again. "Come on, I want to look a little way to the east. I've got a feeling there might be some more growing down that way."

"And they can't be cultivated?" Stu asked as they set off down the slope. "Surely someone must have figured out how to do it. People have figured out how to do *everything* by now."

"Plenty have tried," Fred told him, "but -"

"Hey, what's that!"

Stopping, Stu pointed at a large old mansion in the distance, barely visible beyond the trees.

"I didn't know there was a house out here," he continued.

"That's not a house," Fred replied, immediately sounding a little more concerned. "Come on, there's no need to go that way. We'll take the scenic route that avoids so much climbing."

"But what is it?" Stu asked, still looking in the direction of the house. "It's a big old place. Who lives there?"

"No-one does," Fred explained, "not anymore." He paused for a moment, watching the distant building. "They did once. *Lots* of people lived there back in the day. Holdham Hall used to be a school for orphans, or something like that. Orphaned girls, I think. If I'm not very much mistaken, it was run by a bunch of nuns."

"Is it empty now?"

"It shut down a long while back," Fred told him. "I think there was some... unpleasantness at some point, and the nuns all went away and the place got shut down." He paused again. "To be honest, I'm surprised no-one ever got around to selling it, I'm sure it's worth a pretty penny."

"So why's it empty?"

"I suppose sometimes a house just... dies."

"Dies?"

"You know what I mean. Stories stick. Legends. Rumors. The shadows sort of get ingrained, and suddenly a place has one hell of an atmosphere. That's what happened with Holdham Hall, there was all this gossip about the nuns and their students, and now I don't think anyone would want to buy the house. If they did, they'd never pay what it's worth, so the result is a kind of impasse. Whoever owns it won't sell unless they get a good price, and any buyers are convinced they can sit it out and wait for the owners to change their minds."

"So no-one ever goes there now?"

"Not with the stories you hear," Fred replied as they set off again. "Truth be told, there have always been claims that the house is haunted. And usually when a place gets that kind of reputation, it attracts all sorts of thrill-seekers and ghost-hunters. Not Holdham Hall, though, and do you know why I think that is? I think it's because deep down they know there really *might* be something in that place, and they don't want to meet a real ghost. They just want to scare themselves with a few cheap frights. So on some subconscious level, they stay clear of Holdham Hall precisely because they think there might be something genuinely awful lurking in that place."

The two men continued to talk as they

picked their way further into the forest, leaving any sign of Holdham Hall far behind.

***

Inside Holdham Hall, daylight streamed through the stained-glass windows, picking out thick dust that drifted through the air.

Children had once played on the staircase, but now that staircase stood still and silent. The entire house was empty, save for the furniture that had been left behind many years earlier; paintings still hung on the walls and a vase on one of the tables contained a few dried remnants of some flowers that had died back when people still lived in the house.

More dust drifted through a nearby doorway, into the old assembly room.

On one of the far walls, a long framed photo had been hung many years earlier, showing lots of young girls sitting neatly in several rows on either side of their teachers. This was a school photo that had been taken several decades earlier; all the young girls were doing their best smiles for the camera, some with better luck than others, while a few of the younger girls on the front row looked almost nervously into the lens.

At one end of the front row, one young girl in particular appeared particularly happy. Aged just ten when the photo had been taken, June looked completely carefree, like a young girl filled with hope for the future. She was sitting with her hands resting on her knees, and although the black and white image was a little grainy, any observer would have been able to see – despite the dust on the glass – that young June looked like the happiest girl in the entire school.

A moment later, as more dust drifted past, a hint of movement was caught, reflected in the glass of the frame. Suddenly the glass cracked, and the center of that crack was directly over the image of young June's smiling face.

NEXT IN THIS SERIES

THE SIXTH WINDOW
(THE CHRONICLES OF SISTER JUNE BOOK 6)

The year is 1982. Having survived the terrifying events in the Sahara, June hopes that she's going to be left alone for a while to get on with her life at the convent. Soon, however, she receives a new assignment, and this time her mission is extremely personal.

Many years ago, before she became a nun, June was a scared little orphan at Holdham Hall School for Girls. She and her friend Meredith started investigating claims that the school was haunted, but they soon discovered that ghost-hunting is no child's play.

Now June has been sent back to Holdham Hall, and she's expected to finish the investigation she started all those years ago. She soon discovers that she's not alone, but can anything prepare her for the awful truth of what happened on that terrifying night that set her on the path toward the convent?

AMY CROSS

Also by Amy Cross

1689
(The Haunting of Hadlow House book 1)

All Richard Hadlow wants is a happy family and a peaceful home. Having built the perfect house deep in the Kent countryside, now all he needs is a wife. He's about to discover, however, that even the most perfectly-laid plans can go horribly and tragically wrong.

The year is 1689 and England is in the grip of turmoil. A pretender is trying to take the throne, but Richard has no interest in the affairs of his country. He only cares about finding the perfect wife and giving her a perfect life. But someone – or something – at his newly-built house has other ideas. Is Richard's new life about to be destroyed forever?

Hadlow House is brand new, but already there are strange whispers in the corridors and unexplained noises at night. Has Richard been unlucky, is his new wife simply imagining things, or is a dark secret from the past about to rise up and deliver Richard's worst nightmare? Who wins when the past and the present collide?

Also by Amy Cross

The Haunting of Nelson Street
(The Ghosts of Crowford book 1)

Crowford, a sleepy coastal town in the south of England, might seem like an oasis of calm and tranquility. Beneath the surface, however, dark secrets are waiting to claim fresh victims, and ghostly figures plot revenge.

Having finally decided to leave the hustle of London, Daisy and Richard Johnson buy two houses on Nelson Street, a picturesque street in the center of Crowford. One house is perfect and ready to move into, while the other is a fire-ravaged wreck that needs a lot of work. They figure they have plenty of time to work on the damaged house while Daisy recovers from a traumatic event.

Soon, they discover that the two houses share a common link to the past. Something awful once happened on Nelson Street, something that shook the town to its core.

Also by Amy Cross

The Revenge of the Mercy Belle
(The Ghosts of Crowford book 2)

The year is 1950, and a great tragedy has struck the town of Crowford. Three local men have been killed in a storm, after their fishing boat the Mercy Belle sank. A mysterious fourth man, however, was rescue. Nobody knows who he is, or what he was doing on the Mercy Belle... and the man has lost his memory.

Five years later, messages from the dead warn of impending doom for Crowford. The ghosts of the Mercy Belle's crew demand revenge, and the whole town is being punished. The fourth man still has no memory of his previous existence, but he's married now and living under the named Edward Smith. As Crowford's suffering continues, the locals begin to turn against him.

What really happened on the night the Mercy Belle sank? Did the fourth man cause the tragedy? And will Crowford survive if this man is not sent to meet his fate?

Also by Amy Cross

The Devil, the Witch and the Whore
(The Deal book 1)

"Leave the forest alone. Whatever's out there, just let it be. Don't make it angry."

When a horrific discovery is made at the edge of town, Sheriff James Kopperud realizes the answers he seeks might be waiting beyond in the vast forest. But everybody in the town of Deal knows that there's something out there in the forest, something that should never be disturbed. A deal was made long ago, a deal that was supposed to keep the town safe. And if he insists on investigating the murder of a local girl, James is going to have to break that deal and head out into the wilderness.

Meanwhile, James has no idea that his estranged daughter Ramsey has returned to town. Ramsey is running from something, and she thinks she can find safety in the vast tunnel system that runs beneath the forest. Before long, however, Ramsey finds herself coming face to face with creatures that hide in the shadows. One of these creatures is known as the devil, and another is known as the witch. They're both waiting for the whore to arrive, but for very different reasons. And soon Ramsey is offered a terrible deal, one that could save or destroy the entire town, and maybe even the world.

Also by Amy Cross

The Soul Auction

"I saw a woman on the beach. I watched her face a demon."

Thirty years after her mother's death, Alice Ashcroft is drawn back to the coastal English town of Curridge. Somebody in Curridge has been reviewing Alice's novels online, and in those reviews there have been tantalizing hints at a hidden truth. A truth that seems to be linked to her dead mother.

"Thirty years ago, there was a soul auction."

Once she reaches Curridge, Alice finds strange things happening all around her. Something attacks her car. A figure watches her on the beach at night. And when she tries to find the person who has been reviewing her books, she makes a horrific discovery.

What really happened to Alice's mother thirty years ago? Who was she talking to, just moments before dropping dead on the beach? What caused a huge rockfall that nearly tore a nearby cliff-face in half? And what sinister presence is lurking in the grounds of the local church?

Also by Amy Cross

Darper Danver: The Complete First Series

Five years ago, three friends went to a remote cabin in
the woods and tried to contact the spirit of a long-dead
soldier. They thought they could control whatever
happened next. They were wrong...

Newly released from prison, Cassie Briggs returns to
Fort Powell, determined to get her life back on track.
Soon, however, she begins to suspect that an ancient evil
still lurks in the nearby cabin. Was the mysterious
Darper Danver really destroyed all those years ago, or
does her spirit still linger, waiting for a chance to return?

As Cassie and her ex-boyfriend Fisher are finally forced
to face the truth about what happened in the cabin, they
realize that Darper isn't ready to let go of their lives just
yet. Meanwhile, a vengeful woman plots revenge for her
brother's murder, and a New York ghost writer arrives in
town to uncover the truth. Before long, strange carvings
begin to appear around town and blood starts to flow
once again.

AMY CROSS

Also by Amy Cross

The Ghost of Molly Holt

"Molly Holt is dead. There's nothing to fear in this house."

When three teenagers set out to explore an abandoned house in the middle of a forest, they think they've found the location where the infamous Molly Holt video was filmed.

They've found much more than that...

Tim doesn't believe in ghosts, but he has a crush on a girl who does. That's why he ends up taking her out to the house, and it's also why he lets her take his only flashlight. But as they explore the house together, Tim and Becky start to realize that something else might be lurking in the shadows.

Something that, ten years ago, suffered unimaginable pain.

Something that won't rest until a terrible wrong has been put right.

Also by Amy Cross

American Coven

He kidnapped three women and held them in his basement. He thought they couldn't fight back. He was wrong...

Snatched from the street near her home, Holly Carter is taken to a rural house and thrown down into a stone basement. She meets two other women who have also been kidnapped, and soon Holly learns about the horrific rituals that take place in the house. Eventually, she's called upstairs to take her place in the ice bath.

As her nightmare continues, however, Holly learns about a mysterious power that exists in the basement, and which the three women might be able to harness. When they finally manage to get through the metal door, however, the women have no idea that their fight for freedom is going to stretch out for more than a decade, or that it will culminate in a final, devastating demonstration of their new-found powers.

Also by Amy Cross

The Ash House

Why would anyone ever return to a haunted house?

For Diane Mercer the answer is simple. She's dying of cancer, and she wants to know once and for all whether ghosts are real.

Heading home with her young son, Diane is determined to find out whether the stories are real. After all, everyone else claimed to see and hear strange things in the house over the years. Everyone except Diane had some kind of experience in the house, or in the little ash house in the yard.

As Diane explores the house where she grew up, however, her son is exploring the yard and the forest. And while his mother might be struggling to come to terms with her own impending death, Daniel Mercer is puzzled by fleeting appearances of a strange little girl who seems drawn to the ash house, and by strange, rasping coughs that he keeps hearing at night.

The Ash House is a horror novel about a woman who desperately wants to know what will happen to her when she dies, and about a boy who uncovers the shocking truth about a young girl's murder.

Also by Amy Cross

Haunted

Twenty years ago, the ghost of a dead little girl drove
Sheriff Michael Blaine to his death.

Now, that same ghost is coming for his daughter.

Returning to the small town where she grew up, Alex
Roberts is determined to live a normal, quiet life. For the
residents of Railham, however, she's an unwelcome
reminder of the town's darkest hour.

Twenty years ago, nine-year-old Mo Garvey was found
brutally murdered in a nearby forest. Everyone thinks
that Alex's father was responsible, but if the killer was
brought to justice, why is the ghost of Mo Garvey still
after revenge?

And how far will the real killer go to protect his secret,
when Alex starts getting closer to the truth?

Haunted is a horror novel about a woman who has to
face her past, about a town that would rather forget, and
about a little girl who refuses to let death stand in her
way.

AMY CROSS

AMY CROSS

AMY CROSS

BOOKS BY AMY CROSS

43. Arrival on Thaxos (Dead Souls book 1) (2014)

44. Birthright (Dead Souls book 2) (2014)

45. A Man of Ghosts (Dead Souls book 3) (2014)

46. The Haunting of Hardstone Jail (2014)

47. A Very Respectable Woman (2015)

48. Better the Devil (2015)

49. The Haunting of Marshall Heights (2015)

50. Terror at Camp Everbee (The Ward Z Series book 2) (2015)

51. Guided by Evil (Dead Souls book 4) (2015)

52. Child of a Bloodied Hand (Dead Souls book 5) (2015)

53. Promises of the Dead (Dead Souls book 6) (2015)

54. Days 54 to 61 (Mass Extinction Event book 5) (2015)

55. Angels in the Machine (The Robinson Chronicles book 2) (2015)

56. The Curse of Ah-Qal's Tomb (2015)

57. Broken Red (The Broken Trilogy book 3) (2015)

58. The Farm (2015)

59. Fallen Heroes (Detective Laura Foster book 3) (2015)

60. The Haunting of Emily Stone (2015)

61. Cursed Across Time (Dead Souls book 7) (2015)

62. Destiny of the Dead (Dead Souls book 8) (2015)

63. The Death of Jennifer Kazakos (Dead Souls book 9) (2015)

64. Alice Isn't Well (Death Herself book 1) (2015)

65. Annie's Room (2015)

66. The House on Everley Street (Death Herself book 2) (2015)

67. Meds (The Asylum Trilogy book 2) (2015)

68. Take Me to Church (2015)

69. Ascension (Demon's Grail book 1) (2015)

70. The Priest Hole (Nykolas Freeman book 1) (2015)

71. Eli's Town (2015)

72. The Horror of Raven's Briar Orphanage (Dead Souls book 10) (2015)

73. The Witch of Thaxos (Dead Souls book 11) (2015)

74. The Rise of Ashalla (Dead Souls book 12) (2015)

75. Evolution (Demon's Grail book 2) (2015)

76. The Island (The Island book 1) (2015)

77. The Lighthouse (2015)

78. The Cabin (The Cabin Trilogy book 1) (2015)

79. At the Edge of the Forest (2015)

80. The Devil's Hand (2015)

81. The 13th Demon (Demon's Grail book 3) (2016)

82. After the Cabin (The Cabin Trilogy book 2) (2016)

83. The Border: The Complete Series (2016)

84. The Dead Ones (Death Herself book 3) (2016)

85. A House in London (2016)

86. Persona (The Island book 2) (2016)

For more information, visit:

www.amycross.com

AMY CROSS

Printed in Great Britain
by Amazon